FIVE FOR A DOLLAR

LIBBY HOWARD

CHAPTER 1

The doorbell rang. Cagney began a frenzy of barking, her nails clattering on the hardwood as she tore down the stairs. I raced from the kitchen, dodging boxes and trying to keep Cagney from escaping as I opened the door just a crack to see who it was.

Bert Peter stood on my porch, surrounded by more boxes. He looked down at the brown dog with the black mask trying to squeeze past my legs and grinned.

"Back, Cagney. Get back," I scolded, reaching down to grab her collar with one hand while I opened the door with the other.

"I've got these boxes for the sale," Bert told me before nodding toward the dog. "Is she going to run out?"

"I'll hold her." I scooted Cagney over to the side, told the dog to sit, then held her collar—just in case the excitement of a new visitor overwhelmed her three obedience lessons.

Cagney's tail and rear end wiggled at light speed, but she kept the sit as Bert brought the boxes in and set them with the others in the foyer.

"You've got a lot here," he commented. "Should raise a decent amount of money."

"I hope so." There were more boxes than just those stacked in the foyer. My dining room and parlor were packed, and there were at least two dozen more out in the garage. The town had really come together for the charity yard sale, and I was thrilled—thrilled, aside for the fact that my house had somehow become the collection and staging area of the event.

After the success of Suzette's fundraiser, Matt Poffenberger had roped my friends and me into helping him with his spring charity event—a community yard sale where the proceeds would go toward a Habitat for Humanity project assisting elderly homeowners with much needed repairs. The organization had selected three recipients they decided were in the most need so we could highlight them when soliciting donations and advertising the event. One was a couple who needed a new roof, having somehow survived the winter with a blue tarp covering the rotted section. Another needed a new well pump and some plumbing work as they were having to bathe and fill their toilet tanks with buckets brought up from a nearby stream. The third had a collapsed front porch and window sills so rotted that duct tape was the only thing holding the windows in place.

I remembered how close I'd come to losing my own house just a year ago, how Eli's accident and years of disability had swallowed up our insurance payments, savings, retirement accounts, and even equity in our home. These elderly homeowners...they'd seen disaster after disaster. We were going to do all we could to ensure we raised enough money to provide these people with the home repairs they desperately needed.

"Are these from your uncle's house?" I asked Bert as he brought in the last box. His uncle, Harry Peter, had owned the house across the street from me. Bert had inherited it and although Bert had a home of his own, he'd been in and out of his uncle's house for the last year, going through all the belongings and doing repairs. Harry had been a hoarder, and I was sure the contents of his home would have supplied a dozen yard sales.

"These are from my neighbors in the development," he told me. "Although I did put a few things of Uncle Harry's in this last box. I've already gotten rid of most of his stuff. I'm hoping to list the house for sale next month."

"Wow. That's great," I managed to reply.

I had such mixed emotions at his words. Part of me longed for a new neighbor across the street. Maybe a family with children and pets of their own. I loved envisioning new owners loving the old Victorian and breathing new life into the house. But I still grieved Mr. Peter's death. I still saw the shadowy form of his ghost roaming the porch and passing across the curtainless windows. Taco still went over there daily and yowled at the front door, missing the man who'd always invited him into his home and fed him chicken sandwiches.

But it was time for the old house to be revitalized with new owners. I knew in my heart that Mr. Peter would have wanted that. And hopefully whoever bought the house wouldn't mind Taco pawing at their front door every evening.

"Do you need any help tagging and sorting all of this?" Bert waved a hand at the boxes. "The yard sale is Sunday, right?"

I nodded. "Sunday at the VFW. We're tagging and sorting everything at happy hour tomorrow. You're welcome to come and join in. There's always food plus beer and wine."

I figured that would be the best way to get through all of these boxes of donated items. Combining my traditional

Friday after-work event with some work would take the pressure off me, Daisy, Kat, Suzette, and Olive doing everything on Saturday.

"Oh my gosh, Kay! I'm so sorry." Madison came thundering down the stairs, her noise-cancelling headphones around her neck. "I didn't hear the door. Or Cagney running out of my room."

"It's okay. You're doing homework." I smiled, knowing how hard she was studying for tomorrow's exam. Cagney alternated between her room and Henry's when they were doing homework, then tended to curl up in Judge Beck's bed at night. It wasn't the girl's responsibility to restrain Cagney. The dog was a member of our household now, and we were all making adjustments as well as trying to ensure the hound-mix's obedience lessons were reinforced in the home.

"Hi, Mr. Peter." Madison smiled at the man then turned toward the dog. "Come on, Cagney! Upstairs!"

The dog gave a joyful bark then bounded up the steps, Madison racing after her. The young woman was all long legs and long dark hair. I thought once more of how beautiful she was, the perfect blend of her mother and father's good looks and their tall, slim builds. The girl might bemoan being close to six feet tall at sixteen years old, but I envied her height, as well as her gorgeous hazel eyes—so much like her father's.

"Goodness, she's grown in the past year," Bert commented. "And Henry too. I really appreciated his help going through Uncle Harry's belongings, you know."

I did know, but it was nice how Bert valued Henry's assistance as well as the boy's enthusiastic research on the "antiquities" Bert's uncle had collected. Most of the stuff stacked up five rows deep in Harry Peter's house had been junk, but Henry had found a few items that had been worth enough to pay for the dumpster as well as some drywall repairs. Luckily the house had been paid off, and once sold, Bert would be able to recoup what he'd put into the place plus the considerable investment in time it had taken to clear it out and fix it up.

"I'll try to come by tomorrow night, but I might have to work," he added with a grimace. "Juggling my job with the house renovations has been a struggle. I'll be relieved when I'm done and it's sold. But I'll also be sad when I'm done and it's sold, you know?"

I absolutely knew. "I'll be sad when you're no longer across the street every night and on weekends. Please try to come by for Friday happy hours, though—even after your uncle's house is sold. You'll always be a neighbor and a friend, Bert."

The man's eyes misted a bit at my words. "Thanks for that. I'll admit that I alternated saying a few choice words at my uncle's departed spirit and reminiscing over the past with him while I worked on the place. It will be difficult to put that part of my life behind me for good, but I think it will help coming here and seeing new owners loving and enjoying the house as much as Uncle Harry did."

"Don't let Matt hear you saying anything about missing the work," I teased him. "Before you know it, you'll be reno-vating houses for one charity, and helping clear out hoarder houses for another."

He smiled, but looked thoughtful. "I've actually been thinking of volunteering to help hoarders go through their stuff. Over the past year I'd spent a lot of time wishing I'd been there more for Uncle Harry. I know he had issues besides his hoarding, but maybe if I'd visited more and been supportive instead of criticizing him, I could have made his last few years better. I might not have made much of a dent in his hoarding problem, but I could have at least let him know that I loved him and that he himself was more valuable than all the things in his house."

I appreciated the sentiment, but as much as I'd liked Harry Peter, the man wasn't without his flaws.

"Bert, your uncle threw a toaster at your head. I'm all for better and more forgiving relationships with our friends and family, but it goes both ways, and your uncle wasn't a saint."

He chuckled and shook his head. "Okay. You're right. Isn't it funny how a person's flaws all fade away once they're dead? How they *do* become almost saintly?"

It was true. My own parents and my husband had been pretty close to saintly while they were living, but I tried to remember that they were human. And I was human as well. We all had our bad moments, the things we'd said that we wished we could take back, the things we'd done that we wanted to undo. I believed the key was to love someone, to remember their good deeds and the happy times, but never to forget that none of us were perfect.

"That does seem to be the case." I walked him to the door. "But I was very fond of your uncle. And I'm fond of you too, Bert. You're always welcome here, and I hope you continue to stay in touch."

He smiled back at me as he opened the door. "I hope to. Thanks for your help this year, Kay. I'll see you soon."

I watched him head down the steps, a bit sad at the end of an era. Well, at the end of a year. Harry Peter was dead. All the appliances, boxes, and spare parts were gone from his yard and house. The property across the street still could use a decent landscaping and decorating hand, but it was all neatly trimmed grass, and freshly painted siding. A shadow slid along the porch, clearly visible to my eyes even in the daylight and I smiled.

Rest or wander in peace, Harry Peter, I thought. I also hoped his nephew Bert found some peace of his own as well.

CHAPTER 2

*T*urning around, a rustle in one of the boxes drew my attention. A gray tabby popped his head over the edge of the cardboard, eyeing me before diving back in. Taco was enthralled by all the boxes we now had in our house. He raced between them as if he were in a maze. He loved to hide behind them, darting a paw out to grab at us as we walked by or springing out in ambush. And any box that hadn't been tightly taped closed was fair game for his exploration. I'd need to be careful when transporting all this to the VFW on Saturday morning, or there was a good chance I'd be selling my cat at the charity yard sale along with all this miscellaneous stuff.

"Get out of there, Taco," I scolded.

The cat poked his head up again and I waved the squirt bottle of water at him. But Taco knew I was weak when it came to following through on that particular threat, especially since I didn't want to douse any yard sale items that might be damaged by the water. He eyed the squirt bottle, then vanished back into the box.

I put the bottle aside and went over to get him, finding

the cat buried under a stack of hunter-green damask napkins, and placemats with a pink cabbage rose print.

"Don't go getting cat hair all over the yard sale items," I said as I pulled Taco from the box. He bumped my chin with the top of his head, purring. And with that simple gesture, all was forgiven.

Carrying the cat into the kitchen, I put him down on the floor and checked on the spaghetti sauce simmering on the stove. Taco walked over to his bowl and meowed, eyeing me expectantly.

"You and Cagney have already had dinner," I told him. "It's we humans who haven't eaten yet."

Meow.

"I personally gave you your food—both this morning and this evening. No one has neglected to feed you. You're not starving. In fact, the vet is very upset with me that you haven't managed to lose any weight since your last appointment."

Meow.

"Oh, all right. But just this once." I put the lid back on the spaghetti sauce and reached into the cabinet under the sink where I stashed the dog food, the cat food, and the special treats. It wasn't "just this once." Taco knew I was a softie and couldn't resist giving him treats. I had reduced the frequency and the number of treats I gave him though. And he was getting less dry food in the morning and a smaller can of food in the evening. Hopefully that, along with the new diet cat food, would make a difference in the cat's weight.

As I got a treat from the container, I heard a thump and turned around to see an apple rolling across my kitchen island. Frowning, I picked it up and put it back in the basket with the other fruit, wondering how it had managed to fall out. Taco was on the floor, purring as he weaved in and out of my legs, waiting for his treat, and there was no one else in the kitchen except me.

Bending down I gave the treat to Taco, who took it gently from my hand then tore into it like he was a piranha. There was another thump and I stood to see the apple once more rolling across the counter. As I picked it up, I saw a shadowy figure out of the corner of my eye.

A ghost. My breath caught and for a second I thought it was Eli. I hadn't seen his spirit in months, and although I'd been glad to know he was finally at rest, I missed him and had wanted to selfishly hold him here, to at least have his ghost near me. But this ghost wasn't Eli, and the realization filled me with a strange mixture of relief and regret.

This spirit was a woman—a young woman not much older than Madison. Nineteen? Twenty? I felt a wave of sorrow that someone so young had died, then wondered why this ghost was here, in my house.

I hadn't stumbled across a body, and finding a murder victim usually was the trigger for my seeing a ghost and the ghost following me around. There had been the one time the spirit of a deceased woman had attached itself to a piece of antique furniture that I'd purchased at an estate auction. Maybe this ghost had tagged along with one of the items donated for the charity sale—items that were stacked in boxes all over my house.

I had no idea who she was, what item she was imprinted on, or even if she'd been murdered. From what my friend Olive had told me, sometimes people who died of natural causes stayed behind.

"I can't help you," I told the ghost. Once more an apple rolled out of my fruit basket. I snatched it up before it could fall off the counter and put it back.

"Can't help who?" The shadowy form vanished as soon as

Judge Beck entered the kitchen. He looked around, frowning. "Who were you talking to?"

"Taco," I lied. "He's begging for second dinner."

"Are you a hobbit, Taco?" The judge knelt down and picked up the cat. "Cats don't get second dinner—especially cats who need to lose a few pounds."

"I gave him a treat," I confessed. "I can't help it. I'm a terrible cat-mom. He's just so cute when he begs. And he's not *that* fat. I mean, cats are supposed to be kinda chunky, aren't they?"

"Probably not this chunky." The judge gave me a sympathetic smile. "But Taco has that magical, magnetic, aura. 'Feed me.' 'Give me treats.' I can't resist either."

"Well we need to try harder." I motioned toward the pot on the stove. "The sauce is done. I just need to put the noodles on to boil and we'll be ready for dinner."

"I'll do that if you can take Cagney for a quick walk," the judge said. "The kids are still doing homework, and I hate to interrupt them."

It was Henry's turn to walk Cagney, but schoolwork came first, and I'd come to enjoy the evening walks anyway. When the kids were with their mom, the judge and I alternated dog walking responsibilities. Because I did morning yoga with Daisy, we'd fallen into a routine where the judge got up early, had a quick cup of coffee with us after yoga, then took Cagney for her walk while I showered and got ready for work. The pup got quite a bit of exercise in the morning with the walk and running around the backyard with Daisy's dog Lady, but she was still full of energy when we got home from work and ready to go. I usually got home first and let her out in the backyard for some zoomies while Taco took a stroll around the neighborhood, then it was inside for dinner, and a longer walk after we humans had eaten. Even though I had responsibility for the evening walk, the judge usually came with me, making it a kind of family thing.

On weeks when we had the kids, we still tried to do the family evening walk, but dinner, dishes, homework, and other duties sometimes took priority. We were all still trying to figure out how to make this work, but Cagney was such a welcome addition to our household that she was worth juggling our schedules.

I grabbed the pup's leash, called her down from Madison's room, then fought to get the leash on her collar while she bounced around in excitement.

It was lovely being able to walk the dog while it was still daylight out. Although the dark and the faint glow from the streetlights had been cozy and romantic, it was nice to feel like there was more to the day than only a half an hour after I'd gotten home from work.

Our walk was short since I knew it would only take about ten minutes for the judge to boil the noodles. We came through the door just as Judge Beck was calling the kids down for dinner. It was a simple meal, spaghetti, Italian bread, and a salad, but it was filling and so nice for us all to sit down at the table together.

After dinner, the kids finished their homework while the judge and I put away the leftovers and did the dishes.

"Do you want to start sorting some of these yard sale items, or wait until tomorrow night?" Judge Beck asked once we were done.

"Let's get a head start on it now," I said.

We began opening boxes, designating spots for glassware, household appliances, dishes, linens, and what we were loosely calling decorations.

"Can we help?" Madison asked as she and Henry came downstairs.

The two were eagerly looking at the boxes, especially

Henry. It *was* kind of fun, like opening presents on Christmas morning. Who knew what these boxes contained? And even though we weren't keeping any of these items, it still was fun to see what was inside and to appreciate the goodies we'd hopefully be selling next weekend.

"Have you both finished your homework?" The judge asked his children.

They both nodded.

"Then yes. Just be careful," he warned. "There are breakable items in some of the boxes and they're not all wrapped as carefully as they should be."

We all dove in, sorting and re-boxing like items.

"What do we do if all this stuff doesn't all sell?" Henry asked as he pulled a straw hat out of one box.

I really didn't want to think about that. "Then we bring the items home and decide what to do with them," I told him. "Maybe we can save it all for a second yard sale, or we could donate it. It's up to Matt."

"But where would we store it all?" Madison looked around at the boxes. "In the garage? The basement? We can barely get to the kitchen as it is."

"First, we're hoping it all sells. The things that don't go right away will probably get discounted in the last few hours. And I'm sure Matt has a place to put it all."

I wasn't sure of that. This wasn't a VFW charity event, even though they'd kindly offered to let us use their space for the yard sale. I doubted their generosity would extend to storing dozens of boxes of household goods and linens for months or even a year. Maybe Matt had a storage unit, but I doubted it. A storage unit would cost money and any profit was going to the charity, not toward storing the leftovers. I had a bad feeling that we'd all end up sticking some boxes in our basements and garages until the next sale.

"Oooo, Halloween decorations!" Henry exclaimed as he opened another box. "I might buy some of these myself."

The judge sent him a look filled with horror. "No, you most certainly will not."

Henry was one of those people who believed Halloween decorations should be year-round décor. He had a string of plastic skeleton lights along one wall in his bedroom, and his shelf sported spooky-potion bottles and a set of vampire teeth.

"As long as they stay in your room every month besides October, I'm fine with it," I told him, nearly laughing at the expression of betrayal on the judge's face.

"You could always take them to your room at your mom's," he suggested.

That *did* make me laugh. Poor Heather. I hope she liked fake bloody handprints on her windows and a six-foot tall witch that cackled when you pressed a button, because that's what Henry was examining with serious interest.

"I don't mind if we become the Addams Family house," I teased the judge. "It's a Victorian-style and over a hundred years old. All I'd need to do is paint the outside black and shades of gray, and we'd be set."

"We'd be the talk of the neighborhood, that's what we'd be," Judge Beck countered. "Isn't there a homeowner's association here? I'm pretty sure a black house and Halloween decorations out of season are against the rules."

"I hate to tell you, but there's no HOA here." I laughed at his expression. "But I'm pretty sure the neighbors would stage an intervention. There's quirky, and there's 'Kay has gone off the deep end.'"

"No one staged an intervention for Mr. Peter, and he had dozens of appliances stacked up all over his yard and driveway," Henry chimed in.

"Oh, there were plenty of interventions," I assured him.

"And if you remember, Mr. Lars was very upset living next to all that mess. But Mr. Peter was Mr. Peter, so everyone just learned to live with the junkyard in our midst."

"I'm just saying that if Mr. Peter can have old washing machines and mowers in his yard, you can certainly have a giant, cackling witch in yours," Henry added, as he opened another box. "Ooo! There's bones in this one. Someone really loved their Halloween decorations. I wonder if they upgraded to newer stuff? Or maybe they died and their relatives weren't into Halloween."

My lips twitched, because in Henry's opinion, it would be inconceivable for someone to just decide they didn't want the bother of going all-out every October.

"Just sort the boxes, Henry," Judge Beck scolded "You can shop later, *after* all this is organized and tagged. Actually, you can shop on Sunday like everyone else."

Henry grumbled, but did as he was told, folding the top back on the box and setting it over with the other holiday decorations.

I'll admit that I felt for the boy. It was hard to focus on sorting and stacking, when I also wanted to take a good look at the interesting things people had contributed to the yard sale. One box was filled with silky scarves. Another had handbags—some of them designer. Three boxes held nothing but dozens of novelty coffee cups with different pictures and catchy sayings on them. I found myself wanting to set a few aside to buy, but it wouldn't be fair to do that when Henry had been forbidden from doing the same thing. I'd just have to find a few minutes to wander around the yard sale on Sunday and pick up a few things for myself.

Then I'd smuggle them back home and hope the judge didn't notice. Yes, it was my house, and Judge Beck wouldn't complain if I suddenly brought home six or eight coffee cups, but he'd definitely tease me. And while I didn't mind his teasing, sneaking them in and him not noticing would give me a whole lot of satisfaction.

"Look!" Madison squealed and held up a pair of sneakers. "These are in my size. They're vintage Nike. And they're in great shape."

I didn't get the girl's excitement. They looked like slightly used sneakers to me. But I also didn't get the appeal of a six-foot-tall witch either.

"Madison," her father warned.

The girl pouted, exaggerating the expression with a bat of her long eyelashes.

The judge narrowed his eyes. "That only works when Kay does it."

"Hey." I laughed. "I do not pout. Or bat my eyelashes."

"Maybe you should," he teased.

I felt my face grow hot, still not accustomed to this sort of talk in front of the kids.

"Kay, bat your eyelashes and tell Dad to let me buy these sneakers," Madison said, clearly not bothered about the idea of my flirting with her father.

"If she gets the sneakers, then I get the witch," Henry called out as he came in from the dining room.

The judge sighed. "Fine. You can each pick one item. Put a blue stickie on it, and when we're done pricing things tomorrow night, I'll buy them for you. At this rate, half the charity yard sale stuff won't make it out of our living room."

She and Henry both shouted and pumped a fist in the air.

"Does that include me?" I asked. "I'm thinking three coffee cups equal one pair of sneakers and a giant animatronic witch."

He groaned. "Not the witch. For the love of Pete, not the witch."

"Too late." Henry grinned. "The deal has already been struck and that witch is mine."

"Plus these shoes," Madison added.

"And these coffee cups." I held up three mugs, each with a different saying on them. There had been six I wanted, and selecting only three was difficult. I might have to sneak down later and get the others. It wasn't like I was buying a six-foot tall witch, after all.

"What do you want, Dad?" Madison went to peer over his shoulder.

"Nothing. These are for charity, and we have enough stuff in this house already."

I rolled my eyes. "It's a four thousand square foot Victorian house. If you want a taxidermy squirrel or a walnut suit rack, go for it. It'll be one less thing we have to sell or drag back home to store in the garage, and you'll be paying for it. It's not like you're taking it for free or anything."

"You need that taxidermy squirrel, Dad," Henry teased. "Need."

"I do not need a taxidermy squirrel," the judge countered.

He picked up a golf club from a box and hefted it, hesitating a few seconds before putting it back in the box and sliding the whole thing over to the "sporting goods" section of the room.

I held out the sheet of blue stickers. "You know you want it. Take the golf club. Make it yours. If Henry gets a witch, then you deserve a golf club."

He hesitated, then reached for the stickers. "Okay, I do want it. It's the same brand of sand wedge I lost a few years ago. The right size too."

My eyebrows went up. "Maybe it *is* your sand wedge. Someone picked it up, took it home, and because fate is a wonderful thing, it's found its way back to you via a donation to the charity yard sale."

"I doubt that. I lost it down in South Carolina. I didn't realize it was gone until the next day. I checked and no one had turned it in." He sighed. "I loved that sand wedge. I'm forever leaving them behind, but the loss of that one in particular really stung. I still mourn for it."

I bit back a smile. "And here it is after having traveled hundreds of miles to be reunited with you, just like a faithful dog."

"It *is* the right length for me," he mused, ignoring my comment comparing his lost sand wedge to a dog.

"Fate. Fate. Fate," the kids chanted.

Their father laughed. "Fine. It's mine now. If you all can get coffee cups, used sneakers, and a six-foot witch decoration, then I can treat myself to a sand wedge."

I clapped my hands together. "I'm so happy for you. Congratulations on your new golf club. What are you going to call her?"

The judge eyed the club fondly before putting a blue sticker on the handle. "Sandy. I'm going to call her Sandy."

I laughed. It wasn't the most original name in the world, but it did fit. Sandy, it was.

CHAPTER 3

The next morning the air was clear and crisp. The sun sent peach and golden rays through the slats in the fence and across the yard. Lady and Cagney romped around as Daisy and I did our morning yoga. Taco had insisted on joining us and was perched on the porch railing, eyeing a nearby bird feeder with a twitching tail.

I followed Daisy into a downward dog, looking at the row of red and yellow tulips in the garden. I'd planted them in the fall, and had been thrilled when they'd actually come up this spring. The backyard was looking great, so very different than it had the last few years when nearly a decade of neglect had turned herb and flower gardens into patches of weeds.

Now everything was neat and blooming. Henry had replaced the rotted sections of fence and Madison had painted the whole thing. The hot tub hummed away under a new cover, repaired, clean, and used several times a week—especially when the kids were over.

A year ago I'd been reeling from the loss of my husband, and facing the potential loss of my house. Now I was reasonably financially secure, and with a family to love.

And romance. I thought I'd never love again after Eli passed, but here I was. Strange how something so good could come out of heart-breaking tragedy.

"Did you hear that Peony had her probation hearing and she's due to be released today?" Daisy asked as we shifted into a plank position.

That was one situation that I hoped would result in something good from a tragedy. Peony hadn't meant to kill Holt, but her actions had resulted in his death. It seemed like two lives had been ruined with one stroke, but Peony was young, and I hoped there was some light at the end of this long, dark tunnel for her.

"I knew it was coming up, but I didn't realize it was this week or that she'd be released so quickly." I was happy for the girl, and a bit surprised that Miles hadn't mentioned it to me. Peony's family had refused to allow her to come home after she'd served her time in juvenile detention, and Miles's fiancée, Violet, had agreed to let her sister move in with her. It was a point of tension between the young couple. Miles was a deputy 'with the county sheriff's department. Violet worked for the tax accessor's office at the courthouse and was beginning her master's program in forensic accounting this fall. Violet had her hopes set on a job either with the FBI or in the private, corporate security world. None of that meshed well with having a sister who'd been convicted of second-degree murder, who'd just barely avoided being charged as an adult in the crime.

Peony deserved a second chance, and family was family. I understood Violet wanting to be there for her sister when no one else in her family was stepping up to the plate. But like Miles, I worried that the woman's kindness and generosity might be the thing that derailed her career goals.

"I've gotten her some volunteer hours at the youth shelter," Daisy said. "Thinking I'll start her out with basic housekeeping and helping coordinate group sessions, but I'm hoping she'll be willing to organize activities and even learn to work on the crisis hotline. I've found kids are sometimes more receptive to reaching out to someone near their own age."

"That's a great idea, Daisy." I felt a bit guilty that my friend had been so proactive in keeping tabs on Peony's release and helping her meet her probation requirements while I hadn't even known she'd be out of juvie today. This was Daisy's job and her passion. She loved helping at-risk teens, and I got the impression that Peony's success in probation and in her reintroduction to society would be a huge priority to Daisy. With my best friend and Violet on her side, Peony had a better chance than most kids at making it after incarceration.

"She still needs a paying job though." Daisy shifted from her plank into a cobra pose and I followed her movements.

"Did the thing at the gym not work out?" Molly had mentioned there was an opening at the gym where she used to work. I'd passed the information on to Violet along with a few other openings at local stores and gas stations.

Daisy scowled, taking her cobra pose back to downward dog, then stepping up with her arms at her side in a mountain pose. "The poor girl is being blackballed. No one wants to hire the kid who was convicted of killing our local football hero, even if she's served her time. She's got three months to get a paying job per her probation agreement, and I'm worried."

"I'll keep my eyes open," I told her. "And I'll ask Matt and Judge Beck if they have any ideas. There has to be someone willing to give her a chance."

"I'll keep looking as well," Daisy said, shifting into warrior one. "Lots of my kids struggle with getting that first job.

They don't have a fixed address, or references, or the sort of contacts that make the process easier for other kids. But we persevere, and they do eventually get jobs. The volunteer work helps with their resume, and I know it will help with Peony's too. It's just that she has such a short window of time to get a job before she's in violation of her probation."

"They don't want to send her back to jail," I assured her. "They want her to succeed. If she can show that she's trying and taking positive steps to being employed, they'll probably be willing to extend her deadline."

"I hope so." Daisy shifted into triangle pose. "How did Taco's follow-up at the vet go?"

I glanced at my cat as I mirrored Daisy. "Well, he's still fat. I got the lecture of my life from the vet, and none of my excuses about Taco's sneaking food and excessive napping did any good. He's on some low-calorie kibble now that he hates, and he's not supposed to have any more treats."

"Poor guy," Daisy commented.

I snorted. "Poor Kay. I caved and gave him a treat last night. The 'no treats' thing lasted all of two days."

"He's smart and he's got a good begging face," Daisy pointed out. "It's not your fault you fell under his spell."

"I'll keep trying, but it's hard," I told her. "Plus, I worry that he'll figure out a way to open the fridge in the middle of the night. Or that he'll drive himself to the grocery store for a bag of Happy Cat food."

"Well, if weight is his only issue, that's not so bad," Daisy said. "He's healthy, and in spite of his determined efforts to raid the fridge and steal your leftovers, he'll eventually get with the program and lose weight."

"If only I could get him to join us in yoga." I looked over at the cat who was still perched on the porch railing, tail twitching. "He wasn't so fat when he was outside most of the day, but I just don't feel safe having him running around the neighborhood. It's not fair to the others who live here and have cats or dogs of their own. Or to the birds. And I'm terrified he'll get hit by a car."

"You let him out in the evening before dinner, and when you're in the yard," Daisy pointed out. "That's a decent amount of fresh air. I know people whose cats are indoor twenty-four-seven, and they somehow manage to keep their weight in check. Maybe Taco needs one of those exercise wheels?"

"I'd hoped Cagney would inspire him to run around more," I complained. "Don't get me wrong, I'm glad the puppy isn't chasing Taco and harassing him, but maybe if they'd play together, it would help. A little game of chase wouldn't be so bad. But instead Taco ignores Cagney unless he's trying to steal her food, and Cagney has learned that the cat is grumpy and is a horrible playmate."

"At least they get along." Daisy went back to downward dog, then into cobra once more before shifting into a child's pose.

I eyed Cagney and Lady romping around the yard as I followed her moves. "*Cagney* doesn't seem to have any problems getting in enough exercise." The dog ran around with Lady every morning, then was still bursting with energy for her morning walk. When we got home from work, she nearly toppled us in her eagerness to get out the door for her evening walk. I was in better shape than I'd ever been, and as much as the kids complained, I knew the frequent walks helped them as well.

And Judge Beck was surprisingly into the whole dog thing. He'd confessed that he'd always wanted a dog, but his work schedule had meant that pet ownership would be unfair to both the dog and to Heather who'd be stuck with the majority of the work. Just as he'd stepped up as a parent when he and Heather had separated, he'd also made sure he did more than his fair share when it came to taking care of Cagney. The dog slept on his bed at night. He was the one who was up in the early morning hours when she needed to go outside and relieve herself. Even when the kids took Cagney for her evening walk, Judge Beck sometimes took her out for a second walk.

"Maybe you need to put a harness and a leash on Taco and take him for a daily walk as well," Daisy suggested.

I couldn't help but laugh at the image that conjured up. Taco would flatten himself on the ground and refuse to budge. Instead of dragging him down the sidewalk, I'd end up picking up the cat and carrying him. The exercise would be on my part, walking around the block with an overweight cat in my arms.

"I think the cat-treadmill thing is a better idea. Maybe I could attach a cat toy to it for him to chase, like the greyhounds do at the track. Otherwise I'm not sure he'd use it."

Daisy snorted. "It would probably be Cagney who ended up using it."

"Which still isn't a bad idea. She needs to burn off some of that puppy energy." We both stood and gathered up our mats and towels.

"I'll keep an eye out on those marketplace apps. Sometimes I see stuff like that come up for sale," Daisy said. "It would be a whole lot cheaper to get one used. That way if neither Taco nor Cagney like it, you won't be stuck having paid full price for a giant wheel that just sits in your living room gathering dust."

We walked inside, Daisy calling the dogs and me scooping up my cat to carry him in, well aware that my transporting Taco in my arms wasn't helping his fitness levels.

"You're getting a kitty treadmill," I told him as I set him gently on the floor and got out the bag of cat food.

Taco's enthusiasm over his breakfast greatly diminished the moment I poured the kibble into the bowl. He stared at the brown nuggets, shot me a quick glare, then stared at them once more.

"Sorry, buddy. I know you're outraged at having to eat diet cat food, but I want you to be around for a long time."

The cat sniffed the food, then made a sound as if he were about to cough up a hairball. Daisy opened the back door and both dogs ran in. Lady made a beeline for the water dish, but Cagney paused a few feet from Taco, eyeing the cat's food with longing.

"See? Cagney thinks your new kibble looks tasty," I told Taco.

The cat hunched over his bowl protectively, but still didn't eat any of it. I sighed, taking Cagney by the collar and leading both her and Lady out into the foyer. Taco would eventually eat his food when he got hungry enough and realized that was the only option he had. I still felt bad about the diet kibble, though. He loved his Happy Cat, and I hated not letting him have any. Maybe I could mix the two foods? Would Taco just pick out what he wanted and leave the rest? Or maybe if I mixed them, he'd get used to the new food and the transition would be easier on him.

The dogs ran off for the box of toys. I put up the gate that would keep them out of the kitchen and give Taco as well as us some privacy to eat without two begging dogs, then turned to see Daisy pouring coffee into our mugs.

"Those muffins look amazing," she said as she handed me my coffee.

"Good old-fashioned blueberry," I told her.

"Always a favorite of mine. Although pretty much

anything you make is a favorite of mine." She took a bite and nodded. "Mmm, fresh blueberries."

"I've got lemon pound cake for tonight," I told her. "It's my offer of gratitude for making you all deal with all of this yard sale stuff."

"We volunteered, but the lemon pound cake will be a much appreciated bonus. Holy cow!" Daisy leaned over the doorway gate to peer into the foyer. "Your house is *filled* with boxes! I take it back. Lemon pound cake is a necessity. And wine. There better be a lot of wine if we need to price all of this tonight."

"We *do* need to price all of this tonight, because everything needs to be out of my house tomorrow and down at the VFW," I told her. "I'll be glad to get my house back and not be tripping over stuff every step. And I hope it all sells, not just because I want the charity to make a lot of money, but because I don't want Matt talking me into carting the leftovers back here to store for next year."

"Well I plan on getting some Christmas decorations," Daisy announced. "Looks like you've got quite a lot in that section labeled 'holiday.'"

"We do, although most of it's Halloween stuff. I do think there are some Christmas ornaments and wreathes in there as well." I laughed. "But don't plan on snagging that six-food animatronic witch. Henry has already laid claim to that one."

She chuckled. "Poor you! Is it going up in his room? In the backyard. Has he talked you into putting it on the front porch all year long? And don't give me that face. You're a total softie when it comes to those kids."

I was. But softie or not, I wasn't going have that witch on my front porch all year long. Maybe on special occasions. Okay, I was thinking it could be fun to dress her up and have her on the porch for our Friday happy hours, sort of like a mascot. But that wasn't because I was a softie or anything.

"Right now it's just hanging out in the foyer. Maybe Heather will take a liking to it and Henry can keep it at her house."

Daisy raised an eyebrow. "What are the chances of that happening?"

"Slim to none," I replied. "Is it bad that I'm hoping the witch will have an unfortunate accident requiring a trip to the dump?"

"I'd be praying for that as well." Daisy laughed. "Cagney is in her puppy, chewing phase, isn't she? Would it be possible for her to chew up a six-foot witch?"

Thump.

Daisy and I both turned to see an apple rolling across the kitchen island.

"Poltergeists?" Daisy asked jokingly.

I walked over and replaced the apple. "One with a fixation on apples. She arrived with the charity donations, and I'm hoping she leaves with them as well."

"I wonder what the apple signifies?" Daisy picked it up from the basket and turned it over in her hand. "Didn't Olive say some ghosts attach themselves to objects and locations that were important to them when they were living?"

"She did say that. Usually any poltergeist stuff I've experienced has been because the ghost was trying to tell me something," I replied. "Maybe the ghost had fond memories of apple pies or caramel apples. Maybe she really loved fruit. Or maybe it's just something easy for her to move. I'm just glad she's not knocking pictures off the walls or books off the shelves."

"Well, after tomorrow she'll have to mess with someone else's fruit bowl," Daisy said.

True. Someone was going to buy a scarf or a hat or a lamp and go home with a ghost—a ghost who really liked apples. I felt a little guilty about that. I felt guilty about passing this ghost off on an unwitting shopper. And I felt bad for the ghost.

She'd died young. And she liked apples. What had happened to her? What was keeping here instead of transitioning on to her afterlife?

And what, if anything, could I do to help?

CHAPTER 4

This morning it was Madison's turn to take Cagney for her walk, so I lingered over coffee with Daisy, then enjoyed a leisurely shower and had time for another cup of coffee with the judge before I headed off to work. I arrived ten minutes early, which was pretty close to a miracle given how crazy my mornings had been since we'd adopted Cagney.

Molly came in just as I was setting up the coffee to brew and putting out the blueberry muffins.

"Ooo! Muffins!" she exclaimed.

"Save one for J.T. and one for Miles," I told her. Miles made a habit of popping in a few times each week to mooch baked goods, and it was a good idea to set one aside for my boss as well. The last few days J.T. had been held up and had come into the office late afternoon to find nothing but crumbs. He didn't complain, but I knew he was disappointed when the scones, muffins, cookies, or cakes were all gone.

I wasn't just buttering him up because he was my boss, though. J.T. had been doing all the process serving and repossessions, and that kept him out of the office pretty much the entire day and sometimes well into the evenings. I had dreaded doing the process serving and was glad that those duties hadn't fallen on my shoulders. At least not yet. I was sure as our business picked up, J.T. would ask me to take some of those cases over. For now, Molly and I were doing the research and he was the one lurking around someone's driveway, jumping out of his car, and racing up to them to hand them the papers.

Better him than me. There were things about my investigative job that I disliked and that was one of them. But process serving would be better than the repossessions. J.T. liked to live on the edge, and repossessing cars had gotten him chased, and even attacked a few times. That was one job I absolutely didn't want to do.

About an hour later Miles strolled into the office, a huge grin on his face. The grin widened when he saw the muffins next to the coffee pot.

"One," I told him. "If you eat J.T.'s muffin, then I'm cutting you off for the rest of the week."

He held up his hands. "I'll restrain myself this time, but if you bring in more of those cherry vanilla scones, then all bets are off."

"She brings in those cherry vanilla scones, then there won't be any left for you to eat," Molly told him. "Those are my favorite."

"Clearly I need to start making a double batch of those," I said.

"I recommend a triple batch." Miles poured himself a cup of coffee, and bit into a muffin. "Okay ladies, I've got news. It's time for good/better/best. Which do you want to hear first?"

"Good," Molly told him. "I like to build up to the best. Savor the anticipation a bit."

I nodded in agreement.

Miles let us stew in silence a few seconds as he ate his muffin, building that anticipation. "The good news is that..."

"Go on, we're dying here," Molly groaned,

"Toot's has got the boot," Miles announced. "He's on his way outa here, soon never to be bothering us again."

The sheriff's department had hired Detective Toots roughly a month ago. The moment I'd met the guy, I knew they'd made a horrible mistake. He was abrasive, and an idiot, a caricature of the sloppy, bumbling detective. He'd screwed up the investigation at Suzette's pond, and it was just a matter of time before his ineptitude got someone killed. The guy couldn't leave soon enough, in my opinion.

"Are you sure you didn't lead with the best news?" I asked Miles. "Because I can't imagine topping that one."

"Did Toots get canned?" Molly demanded. "Or shot? Did you deputies all band together and jump him in a back alley or something?"

"No!" Miles eyed her in shock. "We wouldn't...we couldn't... They wanted to fire him, but that's not always an easy or fast solution, so they put him on cold cases while they're getting him another job offer elsewhere that he'll be strongly encouraged to take."

"Kicking that can down the road," Molly commented dryly.

"Sounds like the same situation that resulted in him working here," I added, feeling sorry for whatever town the detective would soon be torturing.

Miles held up his hands. "I don't make the rules, I just celebrate when they work out in my favor. He's leaving. And we'll never be so happy celebrating the departure of a co-worker who'd only been with us for four weeks, two days, seven hours, twelve minutes, and eighteen seconds."

"That's oddly specific," I mentioned to Molly. "I'm getting the impression that Miles doesn't like Detective Toots."

"No one likes Detective Toots—except Detective Toots," Miles said.

"So what's this about cold cases?" Molly asked. "I didn't think the county even had cold cases. Is he looking into an unsolved convenience store robbery from ten years ago? Shoplifting cases?"

"Pretty much. He spent two days grumbling about how his homicide investigative skills were wasted on these petty thefts until he uncovered the Billings case." Miles grimaced. "It's really the only significant unsolved case we have."

Molly sucked in a breath. "*Carly* Billings?"

I frowned, trying to remember an unsolved homicide, and not coming up with anything, although the name Carly Billings did sound vaguely familiar.

Miles nodded. "Carly Billings. Her parents made a police report when she went missing five years ago. At the time, there wasn't much of an investigation. She wasn't a minor, and there was some evidence that led police to believe that she'd just taken off with a boyfriend."

"What changed their mind?" I wondered.

"They found her car dumped in a Walmart parking lot, and it had been vacuumed within an inch of its life. Empty of anything personal at all. Seats and dash bleached. No one goes to that sort of trouble unless they're covering up a crime," Miles said.

"Yes, but was Carly covering up a crime that happened in her car, or someone else?" I wondered.

"It was suspicious enough for us to really start looking for her. And consider the case a potential kidnapping and/or homicide."

"No one ever found her body?" I asked.

"No," Miles replied. "We eventually caught up with the boyfriend down in Florida and he claimed she didn't leave with him—that they broke up a few days before she disappeared."

"The boyfriend could be lying," I pointed out.

"He might have killed her," Molly added.

"If he killed her, he would have to have been really fast about it," Miles said. "The boyfriend gave us a list of hotels he'd stayed at on the way down to Florida, where he'd stopped to eat or for gas, and at one point a buddy he'd visited in Georgia. They all said he was traveling alone, and didn't seem nervous or worried or anything. And he was on the road the night Carly was reported missing. The window of time is really tight if he was the murderer."

"So he killed her and immediately left," I said.

"Then who took the time to clean and dispose of the car?" Molly asked. "Plus, where's the body? He would have been an idiot to drive that distance with it in his car, but maybe that's what he did? And dumped her body in some Florida swamp?."

"So you think he killed her, but was remarkably cool about her body in the trunk during the entire trip?" I asked. "That's pretty psychotic. I'd think even a cold-blooded killer would be nervous about having the cops after him if he'd murdered his girlfriend."

"Not that I was in on the investigation, but I don't think the boyfriend did it. There was no history of them fighting, no controlling behavior, no red flags that her family or her friends saw in the relationship. He was a bit of a deadbeat, but no one pegged him as a violent man—just a lazy one. And from what her friends and her parents said, the boyfriend had been planning this move to Florida for a while," Miles said. "And Carly was debating whether she was going to go or not. That's why they originally thought maybe Carly went off with him, although they said it was unlike her to not let them know she was going, or keep in touch with them after she'd left."

"It *was* unlike Carly," Molly said. "If she hadn't told her parents she was leaving, she would have at least told her friends. *And* given a day or two notice at work."

I turned to her in surprise. "Did you know Carly? Was she a classmate of yours?"

Molly shook her head. "No, but a friend's sister was good friends with her. I've always been a fan of true crime stuff and I asked her about Carly. Plus, this hit close to home. Carly was a Milford girl. Local. That's kinda scary to have someone local just vanish like that, and they never found out what happened to her."

"It is scary," I agreed.

"My friend's sister always insisted that Carly would never run away like that," Molly continued. "Carly didn't do drugs. Her boyfriend was a bit of a loser, but they seemed like a happy couple."

"A happy couple except they broke up a couple of days before she vanished," I pointed out. "Maybe she found a guy who wasn't a loser, and non-violent soon-to-be-ex-boyfriend suddenly got violent when she gave him the old heave-ho?"

"The boyfriend said she'd decided not to go to Florida because she'd gotten a scholarship or something and was going to nursing school," Miles said. "He said it was an amicable split. I know with murders, the husband or boyfriend is the primary suspect, but all this guy's stuff checked out. Plus the timeline didn't work. Carly left her job at seven, and the boyfriend was on a security camera at a place outside of Richmond paying for gas and snacks at nine. At midnight he was in North Carolina grabbing coffee at a truck stop. He couldn't have killed her, disposed of her body, stripped, cleaned, and dumped her car over the Pennsylvania border, then gotten to Richmond in that timeframe."

"I still think it's the boyfriend," Molly said. "Maybe he had a friend help him dispose of the body and the car."

"That's some friend," Miles pointed out. "I don't know about your buddies, but mine aren't going to help me cover up that I murdered my girlfriend."

"True." Molly tapped her lip. "Five years and she was never found, the case unsolved."

"And it will probably remain unsolved, at least in the foreseeable future. I doubt *Detective Toots* is going to make any headway on Carly Billings's disappearance," I drawled. "All he'll probably do is annoy everyone he interviews."

"Enough about the cold case and Toots." Miles pouted. "Does anyone want to hear the other news? The better and the best?"

I laughed. "Yes, we do. Tell us, Miles."

"Yes, tell us." Molly said. "I'm on pins and needles here. Spill the tea, dude."

"Detective Keeler is now ours. Well, maybe ours. The sheriff's department made an agreement with Milford City Police to have him assigned to us temporarily as our lead detective. Actually, he'll be our *only* detective after Toots leaves until we hire a second one, then he'll have the option of staying on as lead detective for the county or returning to Milford."

Molly and I both stared at Miles. I wondered how that bit of news was possibly better than Toots leaving? I respected Detective Keeler. He was smart, competent, and both Locust Point and the county would benefit from his investigative work. But the two of us didn't exactly get along. He saw me as a nosy busybody, and while that was true, I felt I had skills and knowledge that could contribute toward solving our community's crimes.

"That is good news," I finally admitted. As much of a curmudgeon as Keeler was, having him was a million times better than having Toots.

"What's the best news?" Molly asked, clearly as little impressed by Miles' "better" news as I was.

Miles stepped forward, his grin widening. "This deputy right here has signed up to take the detective's exam!"

Molly and I both voiced our excitement and congratulations while Miles broke into a touchdown end-zone worthy dance. When he was done, I ran over and gave him a huge hug.

"I'm so proud of you, Miles! You'll make a great detective," I told him as I stepped back and patted him on the shoulder. This past year I'd grown very fond of the deputy, considering him a good friend. First his and Violet's engagement, and now this. The deputy's life was definitely on a trajectory upward.

"I need to pass the test first," he confessed. "It's not easy. There's a lot to study and there's a chance I won't pass. Even if I do, I'm not sure if the sheriff's department will want to bring on a rookie detective—especially if Keeler decides not to stay. I'd be the sole investigator in the county until they replaced him. I'm not sure I'd be comfortable with that even if the county decided they were."

"But passing the exam means you'll be eligible for a detective job elsewhere," Molly pointed out. "You could move to a city with an entire department of detectives—one that wouldn't have a problem taking on a newbie, where there would be plenty of people to mentor you."

"True, but I really don't want to move, and there's only so far I'd be willing to commute." Miles frowned, his good mood dimming. "Violet works at the courthouse. Unless she got a job elsewhere, we couldn't move. Plus all my friends and family are here. I've never lived anywhere else. I'm not sure I *want* to live anywhere else."

"You've got plenty of time to think through all that," I assured him. "Maybe there will be an opening in Milford—especially if Keeler decides to stay with the sheriff's department. Maybe the county will decide they want more detectives on their force. Plus, you could end up working under Keeler's mentorship."

I might not like the guy, but Miles could learn a lot working with the older detective.

"True." He waved a hand. "But all that's down the road. I have to pass the exam first. I am excited though, and so is Violet. We'll be married. She'll be getting her Master's degree. I'll be a detective." He smiled, looking off into the distance and clearly thinking about his and Violet's future.

This *was* the best news. A young couple in love, starting their life together. Once more I thought of Eli and I, when we were this age and planning our own wedding, our own future.

"So, if you become a detective, does that mean you won't have the time to stop by here every day to eat our muffins and scones, and drink our coffee?" Molly teased Miles. "Because I'm claiming dibs on the extra pastries."

"I'll always make time for Kay's baked goods," Miles told her. "Detective or not. So hands off my muffins."

CHAPTER 5

"*P*ass me more of the red stickers," Violet called out.

Daisy lobbed a roll across the room, and the other woman deftly caught them. Cagney let out an excited bark, running back and forth between the two, hoping for a game of keep-away.

"What are we pricing these?" Kat asked, holding up a blue and tan checked scarf in one hand and a coral paisley one in the other.

Daisy shrugged. "What would you pay for them?"

Kat laughed. "Uh, nothing? I like knitted ones, but silk scarves are not my thing."

"They're *my* thing," I told her. "Two dollars each? A dollar?"

"How about you buy them now and save me the effort of pricing them?" Kat teased, then sighed dramatically at my "no." "Fine. Two dollars it is. Or three for five dollars."

We were all wedged in my house this Friday evening, boxes everywhere. Our usual wine glasses had been exchanged for lidded sip cups to avoid spilling anything on the merchandise. Food was safely kept in the kitchen, and people took frequent short breaks to go grab a bite of cheese, some chips, or a slice of the lemon pound cake.

I hadn't expected quite this many people to show up, especially when they realized how much work they'd need to do for their wine. But everyone was here, cheerfully pitching in to price the yard sale items, box them back up, and haul as much as we could to the garage. At the rate we were going, I wouldn't need to spend tomorrow trying to price items at the last minute.

Tomorrow would be another group effort. We were using the Judge's SUV, a borrowed truck from one of Olive's friends, and both Daisy's and Suzette's small hatchbacks to transport all of these boxes to the VFW. It would take us several trips, then I, as well as any of my friends who were game, would spend the rest of the day unpacking everything and putting it on the tables.

Sunday I'd be at the VFW all day. Volunteers were needed to ring purchases up as well as help keep the merchandise displays neat and orderly. The whole crew would be there, helping coordinate everything and making sure the event went well. Henry, Madison, and Judge Beck had offered to help as well. Madison had her volunteering debut at Suzette's fundraiser, and she had offered to take on the marketing for this event as well as act as the community liaison.

Madison had really impressed me with her dedication and her hard work in making both fundraisers successful. I'd seen her social media posts everywhere advertising the events. They were cute, clever, and if I hadn't been working as a volunteer, I absolutely would have attended as a buyer.

The doorbell rang and Henry scrambled to his feet. "Pizza's here!"

Judge Beck had sprung for dinner in an attempt to keep everyone working as long as it took to get the donations priced and packed. The delivery woman helped Henry carry the boxes to the kitchen, the aroma of garlic, oregano, and cheese wafting through the room in their wake.

"Someone really cleaned out their holiday decorations," Suzette laughed from the dining room. "We've got enough ornaments in this box to decorate the Rockefeller Square tree."

"I might buy a few of those," Olive commented. "They remind me of the ones my grandfather made when I was a little girl."

"And look at this silver tree." Suzette came into the foyer to show us a long forked branch covered with thin metal "needles." "I'm getting a '60s vibe just looking at it."

"A silver tree?" Daisy grinned. "Okay, I'm intrigued. I think there's a picture of me at about two years old in front of a stereo console with a small silver Christmas tree on top."

"Buy it," I teased her. "Buy…it. You know you want to."

"Forget Christmas, I'm in the land of Halloween over here," Kat announced.

"Don't tell Henry," Judge Beck warned. "He already talked me into buying him a six-foot tall animatronic witch. There won't be enough space in his room for him to sleep if he gets any more Halloween decorations."

"Too late," Henry announced as he went over to go through the box with Kat. "I didn't go through *this* box last night. Ooo, there's a jar of plastic eyeballs in here!"

"I'm tempted to buy those myself." Kat laughed as Henry handed her the jar of eyeballs and dove into the box. "Can I admit to an addiction to those plastic animal skeletons? I've got a cat, a dog, a crow, a dozen rats, and a flamingo. None of them are truly correct since the manufacturer made the cartridge parts 'bone' so they'd be easily identifiable, but I still love them."

"Flamingo?" I laughed. Hellhounds, black cats, crows, and rats all sounded very Halloween-y to me, but *flamingos*?

"Oh, you just wait until this October. I plan on having a yard full of skeleton flamingos," Kat said.

Henry rustled around in the box for a second then popped his head up. "Uhhh, Miss. Kay?"

"What?" I brushed my hands against my pants and made my way toward the foyer where they was working. "What did you find? An actual rat?"

"Ewww," Madison said from behind me.

"No. Not a rat."

As I walked into the foyer I saw Henry holding a skull as if he were playing Hamlet in a community theater production.

I'll admit my first thought was that we couldn't let Henry buy this. A six foot tall animatronic witch was bad enough, but I didn't want skulls and bones all over my house—especially ones this realistic.

"Kay," Kat said, her voice quivering a bit as she took the skull from Henry. "I...I don't think this is fake. I think it's a real skull."

CHAPTER 6

"*I*s it real?" I asked Judge Beck.

We were all crammed into the foyer, passing the skull around so that each of us could examine it.

The judge shrugged. "They didn't cover this kind of thing in law school, so I've got no idea."

"I...I think it's real." Suzette shivered and passed the skull to Olive.

She held it in her hands, looking into the eye sockets intently. Olive might be a suit-wearing accounting manager during the day, but she was also a medium and able to communicate with ghosts.

A shadowy form materialized behind her. My gaze shifted to the spirit, but as always the ghost was indistinct and remained just outside of my direct vision.

It was a woman—a young woman. And she was frightened.

Olive drew in a ragged breath. Her eyes met mine as she passed the skull to Violet.

"I think it might be real as well," Violet said, absolutely unaware of what Olive and I had seen. Or felt.

Violet passed the skull to Miles who abruptly sent it on to me.

"If it's real, then what should we do with it?" I looked at Miles. And he held up his hands.

"If someone turns up human remains when plowing their field, we show up, and watch while the Medical Examiner's office does their thing," he told me.

"That happens?" Violet asked, her voice raising in pitch. "How often does someone turn up a body while they're plowing a field?"

"Pretty much never," Miles admitted. "But it has happened. People have family cemeteries on old farmland, and the stones get moved, or generations later people forget where the family graveyard is. Or it gets sold to development, and there was no record of the family cemetery. That happened over in Halfort County a few years ago."

"That's creepy." Violet shivered.

"But we didn't turn this up in a field," I pointed out. "We turned it up in a box of donated Halloween decorations. And while it certainly seems like an actual human skull, none of us know that for certain. I'm sure there are plenty of companies out there making some plausible fakes for movie sets or haunted houses, or quirky decorations."

"That would be Henry, having those quirky decorations," Madison chimed in, elbowing her brother.

"Do you want me to take it in and give it to the ME's office?" Miles asked. "It's your call. I don't know how long it will take them to get to it, though."

"Maybe I can have someone look at it first. Just to make sure it's real before I go wasting police resources," I mused. "I wonder who to go to?"

"My friend Carlotta is a nurse," Olive spoke up. "Maybe she could tell if it was real?"

"Or Tammy," Suzette suggested. "She's an archeologist."

"If it's not a pottery shard, I don't think Tammy can help," Olive said. "But it might be worth it to call her. I'll bet she knows someone."

"If it turns out to be real, should we make a police report?" I wondered. "Is it illegal to own human remains?"

Again we all looked at Miles then at Judge Beck.

"The only reason I know this one is because of a weird case I read about that took me down a research rabbit hole," the judge told us. "Up until the latter part of the twentieth century, human skeletons were regularly imported for use in medical studies. Due to changing laws in the exporting countries, the companies that sold these switched to replicas instead."

"Wait, so like forty years ago people could just buy a real human skeleton?" Madison asked.

"At that time, a lot of medical students were required to purchase one," the judge told her.

"That's sick," Henry commented.

"Yeah, sick as in gross, not sick as in cool," I told the boy.

"Although there is currently no way to legally obtain *new* human skeleton remains, there are thousands of these older skeletons in the country still in private hands. For those, there is no law regulating their distribution, sale, or ownership. Unless you live in Louisiana, Tennessee, or Georgia, that is. Ones belonging to museums or universities or research facilities cannot be sold, only transferred to other facilities, but ones in private hands can be sold." The judge stepped back, hands raised, and we all clapped at his recitation of weird legal trivia.

"Who else is dying to hear the actual legal case that sent Judge Beck down this rabbit hole of research?" Daisy asked. "Was someone trying to profit by robbing graves? Save money on funeral expenses by selling Uncle George's bones to the neighbors?"

Judge Beck chuckled. "Nothing so interesting. It had to do with a university program that was closing and their disposal of the bodies used in high level anatomy and pre-med classrooms and labs."

"I wonder how many bodies they had," Henry said. "Were they just skeletons and parts in jars, or actual whole bodies?"

"Yuck." Madison wrinkled her nose. "I don't want to think about that. Let's change the subject."

"Guess your daughter isn't heading for medical school then," Matt joked to Judge Beck.

"No, but I'm now thinking Henry might be." The judge laughed.

"Well, legal or not, I don't feel comfortable putting actual human remains in a yard sale," I said. "It just seems wrong to be profiting off of Uncle George, or whomever, even if it's for charity."

"We're not even sure if it's real or not," Daisy reminded me. "If the skull is a really good reproduction, made to be used in a medical schools or doctor's office, then it would be hard for us to tell the difference. It could just be a good fake."

"Do you want me to take it in?" Miles offered. "I can file a report and drop it off at the medical examiner's office."

I thought about that for a second, hating to waste both Miles's and the M.E.'s time when I could cut out all the middle men and women and take the skull straight to the person they'd probably end up consulting anyway.

"No, I think I'll do some research myself before I do anything official. Thanks for the offer though," I told Miles before I turned to Olive. "You said you have an archeologist friend? And that she might know a forensic archeologist?"

Olive nodded. "Do you want me to call her and set up a meeting?"

"I'd appreciate it. If it's fake, then I'll just be embarrassed, store it in the attic, and we can sell it at next year's yard sale.

If it was for medical use, then I'll find somewhere we can donate it that won't feel like we're profiting off someone's skeleton. If there is any question about it being from a grave, then I'll turn it over to the police."

"Just the skull, or these bones as well?" Madison asked, holding up what looked like a femur.

I winced. "Let's put all the bones that aren't obviously plastic or foam in this box over here. If I'm going to visit a forensic archeologist, then I might as well have them look over the whole lot."

We put them gently into the box, then went back to work. All evening I kept seeing the shadows of a ghost out of the corner of my eye. As much as I hoped the skull and other bones were fakes, her presence told me otherwise.

Maybe there was a good reason for a woman's skull to be in a box of Halloween decorations that had come from someone's attic.

Or maybe not.

CHAPTER 7

*I*t was late when we finished up pricing, re-boxing, and sorting all of the donations. We piled as many boxes as we could into the garage, leaving the rest of them in my house. Then I said goodbye to my friends and waved them off, knowing I'd see most of them tomorrow morning to cart all of this stuff over to the VFW.

There was no family dinner tonight since we'd all eaten pizza and snacks during our work. Exhausted, I wandered inside to see the judge, Henry, and Madison at the dining room table. Madison was typing on her phone, her expression rapt as she eyed the screen. The judge was sorting through stacks of papers, his laptop to the side. Henry was eyeing his tablet.

I sighed, hating that we were doing work on a Friday night. Well the judge appeared to be doing work, anyway. The kids were messaging their friends or playing games. But I was just as bad as the judge when it came to work. In fact, I had some files clamoring for my attention in my bag right now, but I was going to resist at least until Sunday when the kids went back to Heather's house.

Judge Beck normally did the same. He prioritized his children when they were at our house, but his job still filled more than an eight-hour day, and occasionally he'd burn the midnight oil after the kids went to bed, sacrificing sleep to keep a precarious work-family balance.

I hesitated, then went over to him, wrapping my arms around his neck and leaning myself against his back. "Busy week?"

It had taken me a while to get used to physical affection with him in front of his children, let alone in front of our friends, or even strangers. But he'd made it clear that our relationship wasn't something he wanted to hide, so I wasn't going to hold back on casual demonstrative actions.

"It was a busy week." His hands came up to grip my arms, holding me against him. "But I'm just going to take a quick look at these papers and type a few e-mails. I'll have a more relaxed weekend if I get these out of the way."

"Then I'll go with Madison and Henry to take Cagney for a walk." I looked over at the two. "Unless they're busy with homework."

Madison shot me a guilty glance. "Just messaging friends about the lacrosse game next week. Let me change my shoes and I'll be ready for a walk."

"I'm doing research," Henry announced. "Not homework research, though. It's bone research, because of the skull we found."

"Ugh," Madison announced with an eye roll as she headed off to change her shoes.

"What did you find out?" I asked Henry.

"That skulls are expensive," He turned the tablet to face us. "There are osteologists that work with bones. This company sells skeletons that were previously used in medical schools. They're all over a thousand dollars each!"

I bit my lip, wondering if I'd made the right decision on

not to sell the skull or other bones. Even if we sold them for half the going price, it would be a significant amount of money for our charity.

"This place says they'll buy bones as well," Henry added. "So if you don't feel right having them out on display, you could always privately sell them."

"It's a good idea," Judge Beck said. "It feels more respectful that way."

"Let me think about it. I really want to get the all-clear from the local authorities first, then if it turns out this is a skull and bones from a hospital or university, we'll consider selling them to a legitimate organization." I looked over at the box holding the remains. "I just wish we could figure out who donated them. They'd be able to tell us how they came to have the bones. I'd feel a lot better about them if I knew they were honestly acquired."

"I think you've done enough research about bones and skulls," Judge Beck told his son. "Go walk the dog, and when you're back, I'll make us all milkshakes."

Henry jumped to his feet. "That's a deal!"

With all the preparation for our yard sale, happy hour had run past sunset. We'd gotten used to walking Cagney in the dark the last few months, and the street lights made a pleasant glow on the sidewalks and the yards as we strolled. We took our usual six block circuit, chatting about the upcoming charity event, school sports, and a new video game Henry was obsessed with. Back home, we enjoyed chocolate milkshakes and watched a movie.

Judge Beck and I cleaned up the kitchen after the kids went to bed. The pair of us worked in companionable silence, and my thoughts turned to the skull, to the yard sale, then to my morning yoga session with Daisy.

"Daisy said that Peony is out of juvie," I mentioned to the judge as we dried the tall milkshake glasses. "I don't know if she'll be going back to school or not, but I figured Madison might at least run into her, even if they don't continue their friendship."

The judge sighed. "I've been thinking about that. Madison wrote to her while she was in the detention center. I'm not sure if Peony wrote back or not, or what the status of their friendship is, but I know Madison is open to picking things up where they left off."

"She's loyal and forgiving," I told the judge. "And Peony will need friends like that."

He put the glasses in the cabinet and turned to face me. "I know. And I'm a horrible person for hoping their friendship dies and they drift apart. I didn't think they had a lot in common before Peony was convicted, and they have even less in common now."

"You're not a horrible person, you're just a father who wants the best for his daughter," I pointed out. "But Madison is sixteen. She's sensible and smart, and I think you can trust her to back away if Peony tries to embroil her in any trouble."

He shrugged. "I know that, but I also remember that last year we caught her going to a party with college-age kids, with alcohol and quite possibly drugs—a party where a woman was recruiting young women for an escort service. She was actually approached to participate in the prostitution ring. That wasn't exactly good judgement on her part."

"It wasn't good judgement for her to attend that party, but I did the same at her age. She didn't do drugs. She didn't do more than sip her beer. She didn't fool around with any of the boys. And she didn't end up an escort. That sounds like good judgement to me."

He bit back a smile. "Underage drinking is illegal. Sipping a beer at fifteen isn't good judgement."

I rolled my eyes. "Okay Mr. Straight-laced. Personally I

don't see anything wrong with sipping a beer as a teen, but I'm not her parent. You win on that one. And you win on the party. But didn't she learn from that lesson? She's been the model of a mature, responsible young woman ever since. At what point do you start to trust again?"

He stepped forward and put his arms around me, pulling me against him. "You're right. And if she wants to be friends with Peony again, I will trust her. I'll even let her invite Peony over for dinner or to study."

"To *my* house? How generous?" I teased.

"That's me. Mr. Generous."

He leaned down and kissed me. And I felt all the butterflies and heart-skipping that I used to feel as a teenager. I kissed him back, my arms around his neck, holding him tight.

And then we went to bed. Alone. In separate bedrooms. Because his children were here this week, and we were taking things slow.

Although I was beginning to wish we weren't taking things *quite* this slow.

CHAPTER 8

I was up early on Saturday, brewing a pot of coffee and ready for sunrise yoga when Daisy came through the back door. One look at her face and I knew something was wrong

"What is it?" My heart raced as I glanced at Lady, who looked perfectly fine, dancing around the kitchen as she greeted Cagney and a grumpy Taco. Had J.T. had an accident? Or one of our friends?

"Kay, your garage...you've been robbed," Daisy blurted out.

My immediate reaction was relief. Buildings could be repaired and stuff replaced. Thank God nothing had happened to one of our friends.

"The garage?" I asked, Daisy's words sinking in. "There's nothing in there to steal except some tools, and an ancient mower. And some of the yard sale stuff."

I doubted anyone would want to steal donated scarves and 1980s skinny ties, but who knew? The bad thing would be if we needed to re-sort and label the donations before hauling them all over to the VFW for the yard sale.

"I can't tell if anything was taken or not, but they sure made a mess of the place. I think you need to call the police."

I grimaced. "That bad, huh?"

"It might not be *so* bad," Daisy replied. "It was probably just kids looking for change or something to pawn, but even if they didn't take anything, it's still vandalism. And there should be an official report in case this sort of thing happens again."

Ugh. I hated the thought of our little town and our sleepy street becoming a crime zone, but Daisy was right. There weren't a lot of teens in this neighborhood, so the residents needed to be on the lookout for cars and pedestrians in the area late at night or early in the morning.

Just to be on the safe side, I leashed Cagney before I grabbed my phone and headed out back. Daisy followed me, Lady also leashed. The garage was a mess. Eli and I had never gotten around to installing an electric garage door opener since we only used the one-car building for storage. We'd never bothered to lock it either—something I clearly needed to remedy. The culprit had slid the door halfway open without any of us even hearing it, and had tossed the place. Tools were knocked off the shelves and scattered on the floor. The neat boxes for the yard sale had been opened with the contents strewn about. The ancient mower was still there in the corner, and a quick glance had me believing that the would-be robbers had left disappointed and empty-handed.

After telling the 911 operator what had happened, I hung up and shook my head, annoyed that I was going to spend the morning cleaning all of this up instead of having a relaxing yoga session with Daisy.

It wasn't easy resisting the urge to start cleaning the mess up, but I managed to restrain myself until the police arrived. To their credit, they drove quietly down our street and into our driveway, lights and sirens off. Miles got out of his cruiser, another woman I recognized as Cheryl Bauer-schmidt climbing out of the second cruiser.

"Miss Kay." Miles jogged up to me, giving both Lady and Cagney a quick pat. "When I heard the call, I came straight over. Is everyone okay?"

"So okay we didn't even know we'd been robbed until Daisy came by for yoga," I joked. "It's just the garage. No one tried to get into the house—that I'm aware of, anyway."

"I'm sure if someone had tried to get into the house, Cagney would have alerted you," Miles replied.

I shrugged. "Maybe. Or she might have just run down-stairs and licked the intruder to death. You might have been investigating a death by puppy this morning instead of a vandalism."

"They didn't take anything?" Cheryl asked, squatting down to greet the two dogs.

"I'm not sure. I didn't want to touch anything until you got here," I told her.

Miles surveyed the mess, shaking his head. "Probably just kids looking for something to pawn for booze money. We'll file a report and watch for any trends of break-ins, but there's a good chance we'll never catch the perps—especially if this was just a one-time thing."

"We'll dust for prints on the door, but it's a long shot. Even if we get more than a partial, chances are there won't be a match in the system." Cheryl walked up to stand beside Miles. "Imagine the guts it takes to break into the garage at a judge's house."

"Kids wouldn't know Judge Beck lives here," Miles told her. "Not unless they're friends of Madison's or Henry's, and I doubt any of *their* friends would pull something like this."

"So how should we do this?" I asked the two deputies. "Am I free to go ahead and sort through the wreckage while you dust for prints?"

They both nodded. Daisy and I put Cagney and Lady into the fenced backyard to play while the two of us got to work sorting and re-boxing the donations. I was well aware that "dusting for prints" wasn't a normal procedure for minor vandalism where damage was minimal and it didn't seem like anything had been stolen. No doubt the fact that Judge Beck lived here played into Miles and Cheryl taking extra care and effort with the crime scene.

We'd made a decent dent in cleaning up the donations when Judge Beck appeared, still in his Hello Kitty pajamas that Madison had bought him and a threadbare T-shirt, a coffee cup in his hand.

"What's going on?" he asked, stifling a yawn. "I looked out the window, and saw the cruisers."

"Someone tossed your garage, Your Honor," Cheryl said with a nod that was darned closed to a bow.

I hid a grin, thinking of how law enforcement tended to treat Judge Beck as if he were royalty. Not that I blamed them. I'd been intimidated by the judge the first day I'd met him. It still felt unreal that we were dating. Everything from my heart down heated up at the thought. Dating and hopefully more. A month of kissing and affection had been slowly moving toward increased intimacy. The glacial progress of our physical relationship was partially due to us having Judge Beck's kids every other week, partially due to him being recently divorced and me being recently widowed, *and* the fact that Cagney slept at the end of his bed.

The kids knew we were a couple, and heartily approved. I was pretty sure Cagney approved as well, but I didn't really want a canine spectator when we got to the point of making love. And to be honest, the slow build up had ratcheted my libido to a level I hadn't believed possible. The kids went back to their mother's house Sunday night, and I was hoping this week would be *the* week. But his bed or mine? Would

Cagney whine and scratch at the door the entire time? Maybe I needed to get her a bone to distract her. Should I buy new underwear? Maybe a bra that wasn't ten years old?

Judge Beck stiffened at Cheryl's comment. His gaze sharpened as he looked around the garage before it landed on me. "You okay?"

Heat raced through me once more. He wasn't worried about his car or the garage or the donations. He was worried about how *I* was feeling about the whole thing.

"I'm fine. Honestly it was probably just a bunch of kids randomly hitting an old unlocked garage without an electric opener. These things happen." I squirmed a bit under the intensity of his gaze.

"I think we need a security system. Both for the house and the garage," he announced

"It wouldn't hurt," Cheryl said.

"It's overkill," I protested. "There hasn't been more than one or maybe two robberies on this street since I've moved in. I'm sure this isn't a trend or anything. We don't need a security system."

"I don't like this, Kay," the judge said. "One-off or not, I don't like this."

I held back an eye roll. "We have Cagney. And an attack cat. We don't need a security system."

"Cagney is a puppy," he countered. "And she's more likely to happily greet any intruder than scare one off. And Taco will dart between the robber's legs to go explore outdoors. We need a security system."

"From what I can see they didn't steal anything. If you want a security system, then fine. But just be aware that I'll be forgetting to set it, or accidentally tripping it all the time."

"That's a chance I'm willing to take. I don't like waking up to find two sheriff's department cruisers in the driveway and a tossed garage."

I gave him a reluctant nod. If he wanted a security system, then so be it. I knew he'd pay for it, which was good since I certainly didn't have the budget for that sort of thing. Judge Beck faced criminals and the justice system every day. That had to make a person hyper-aware of crime. If putting in some sort of electronic security made him feel better, then I wasn't going to fight over it.

"Got some prints," Cheryl announced, breaking the tension between me and the judge. "We'll need to get everyone's prints to rule out those who actually live here. Hopefully we've got one or two from the actual perp."

I thought of everyone who'd helped last night and winced. "It's not just the judge, me, and the kids who've had access to the garage over the past few days," I told her. "These boxes are full of donated items for a charity yard sale. We had a bunch of people over last night to tag and sort them, and quite a few of them helped take these boxes to the garage."

Cheryl eyed me. "How many people are we talking about here?"

I mentally counted. "Ten? Twelve?"

The deputy sighed. I gave her a reassuring smile, knowing that she and Miles were doing their best.

"Nothing seems to be broken or missing," Daisy announced from the back part of the garage. "Although I'm not sure if I'd know that a twenty-year-old blender or a toaster from the '70s was missing or not."

"I can't see that anything's missing either." I glanced up at the judge. "It was probably just some kids. There's nothing stolen, nothing damaged. I don't want to overreact about this."

A muscle twitched in his jaw. "Well, I do. We're getting a security system, and some new locks. I don't like this. I don't like this at all."

* * *

I⊤ DIDN'T TAKE Daisy and me long to finish cleaning up the mess in the garage. We ended up skipping yoga, instead going into the house for some coffee and breakfast courtesy of Judge Beck. After we'd shooed him away from the crime scene, he'd gone inside and made us all French toast. By the time Daisy and I were done in the garage, the kids were up and we all sat at the dining room table and ate while the dogs had their kibble and Taco loudly protested that no one had fed him in weeks, even though I'd given him his breakfast before Daisy had arrived.

The kids cleaned up the dishes while the adults began to load boxes into the judge's SUV and my sedan. A few moments in, Kat, Suzette, and Violet arrived and began putting boxes into their vehicles as well. Violet snagged my sleeve as I walked by, pulling me to the side.

"Miles texted me to say you'd had a robbery. Kay, are you all right? That's so scary!"

"Someone got into my unlocked garage and tossed it," I patted her shoulder. "Nothing was stolen, or broken. Everything's fine. It was probably just kids. No big deal."

Violet shuddered. "Doesn't that totally freak you out? Someone was here, right outside your house. They were breaking into your garage, going through your stuff while you were sleeping."

"*Now* I'm freaked out," I teased her. "Thanks for that. No one was hurt. Nothing was stolen. They didn't even break the garage door. If I know Judge Beck, he'll have cameras all over the place by the end of the week. And a daily drive-by police presence."

"You're right," she said, not looking convinced. "My apartment is in a good neighborhood, but things still happen. I know I feel better when Miles sleeps over. And Starsky."

I laughed at that. Miles had adopted the largest and laziest of the rescue puppies Daisy and I had found homes for. Starsky's size might be intimidating, but the dog would probably keep on sleeping through any robbery. Not that his littermate Cagney was any better. I was happy we had a cheerful and friendly pup, but this was the tradeoff. Neither would ever be a guard dog.

We made four trips back and forth to the VFW, then on the final trip, we all stayed to unload and organize the sale items on the tables. A few of the pricing stickers had come off in transit and during the unboxing, so I had to wing it, sticking what I assumed was the correct price on each item. Matt showed up at noon with sandwiches, chips, and sodas. After a quick break, we were at it again, trying to get everything done before dinner.

"Kay?" Violet approached me, biting her lip and twisting the hem of her T-shirt in her hands. "I wanted to ask you if it would be okay for me to bring Peony tomorrow. She doesn't have any volunteer shifts, and I hate to leave her home alone all day so soon after getting…out. She can help with the sale if that's okay. Make sure the tables are clean and neat, that stuff is organized. I get it if you don't want her running a cash register or helping customers."

My heart went out to the girl and her sister. Peony had to be feeling self-conscious and worried about how people might react to her presence. I was sure she'd rather remain in Violet's apartment, hidden away and watching television all day, but Violet was right to want her to get out in public as much as possible. It would be hard at first, but this was the only way. She needed to get through the difficulty of returning to society after her time in juvenile detention—and do it now rather than draw it out. People would never get beyond her crime and the past if she hid herself away.

"We'd welcome her help," I told Violet. "I think we're okay

with the registers, but if she feels comfortable helping customers that would be great. If not, we definitely could use the assistance keeping everything neat and organized. I've seen how people are at these yard sales."

Violet smiled, her shoulders relaxing. "Thanks. She's having a tough time transitioning. Her having things to do helps. I really appreciate Daisy lining the volunteer work up for her. Oh, and I forgot to mention! She starts at the shelter next week, cleaning pens and doing some administrative work. It's only ten hours a week, but it's a paying job and it'll satisfy her parole requirements. Plus, she is really looking forward to it. We just need to figure out how to get her a car. I can't keep driving her everywhere with my work schedule, and the bus service in town is pretty lame. She's willing to walk or even bike to work and to her volunteer job at the youth center, but the weather doesn't always cooperate with that. We can only afford so many Ubers."

I wasn't sure how to reply to all that. "I'll keep my eyes open for an inexpensive car. Is there someone at the shelter she can carpool with? Until she gets a ride of her own?"

"We're working on that." Violet brushed a hand over her eyes. "I'm sorry. I didn't mean to dump all of that on you. It's just I don't have anyone to talk to. I don't want Peony to think she's a burden. The girl has enough she's dealing with right now. And Miles...well, Peony is a bit of a touchy subject with him. He listens, and I know he tries to be supportive, but the man has the worst poker face ever. I know he doesn't approve, and that he wishes she was anywhere but at my apartment, that she wasn't my responsibility. But she's got nowhere else to go, and the terms of her parole stipulate she needs a place to live and at least part-time employment or school."

"You don't need to apologize for needing an ear to talk to. That's what friends are for," I told her. "I think you're wonderful, doing all of this for your sister. I just hope you and Peony have some sort of transition plan in place, because it isn't fair for you to have responsibility for her long-term."

"Plans are a bit fluid right now." She gave me a rueful smile. "We're just trying to get through her parole period, get her some cash as well as a decent job and a car. From there we can think about her renting a small place of her own."

"What about school?" I asked, feeling for the sisters. "Is she going to go back to high school? Or taking her GED? What about college?"

Violet sighed. "Peony is smart enough to go to college. She got good grades. I know she could get her degree, but right now she's not confident in her ability to pursue anything as far as higher education goes. I can't even talk her into going back to high school. I think she's embarrassed to face everyone after missing a year of school—especially since everyone knows what happened and where she was last year. My goal is to talk her into taking her GED in the next year or two, but I think college might be out of the question for her."

That was so sad. But there was plenty of time for Peony to go to school later. Several of my college classmates had been freshmen in their mid-twenties or even older. Of course, there were plenty of careers that didn't require college. And who knew how the girl would feel in a year or two. She'd only *just* been released. She needed time to adjust.

CHAPTER 9

Sunday morning I was up before the sun again, except Daisy and I were once more skipping our pre-dawn yoga, this time for the yard sale. As proud as I was of all the hard work we'd put into this event and the money it would generate for the charity, I would be glad when it was all over and I could get back to my routine.

After a quick shower, I raced downstairs and was surprised to see that Judge Beck was already in the kitchen, pouring coffee into go-cups as well as a giant thermos. He had a cooler packed with snacks, sandwiches, and drinks even though there would be concessions at the yard sale. Madison and Henry were also up, both heavy-eyed and yawning as they poured food into both Cagney's and Taco's bowls.

"I bought donuts," he said, pushing a box of store-bought crullers my way. "I know it's not up to your muffin-and-scone standards, but I figured Krumpe's was better than anything I could make myself."

"I love Krumpe's." I dug one out of the box. "And they're warm! When did you get up this morning?"

"Three." He shot me an embarrassed smile. "I couldn't sleep. That thing with the garage yesterday really bothered me. I tossed and turned and finally got up and went out for donuts. Cagney was upset I didn't take her, but I didn't want to leave you and the kids with only Taco to defend you from intruders."

I bit into the donut, enjoying the firm dough and sugary bliss of the cruller. "I'm surprised you left us to Cagney's questionable guard dog skills instead of just staying here yourself."

"Trust me, I thought long and hard about that. Those cameras better be here by the end of the week because I'm probably going to be a sleepless wreck until they're installed. I managed to convince myself that Cagney could keep you all safe in the thirty minutes it took me to go get donuts and come back here."

"You're putting a lot of faith in a happy, friendly puppy," I teased him. "But I'm glad you got the donuts. I haven't had a spare moment to bake and the blueberry muffins and lemon pound cake are gone."

"Should we put Cagney in the crate while we're gone?" Henry asked, placing the dog food in the cabinet under the island.

I thought about that for a few seconds. Cagney was still a puppy and prone to some destructive behaviors. I hated crating her for the day, but the last time she'd been left loose for the day I'd come home to two shredded dish towels and all the sofa cushions removed and in random locations throughout the house. The time before she'd managed to get a bag of potato chips off the counter and shred the bag. I wasn't sure if Cagney or Taco ate the chips. Judging from the gastric distress that evening and the next morning, I was guessing they'd shared.

"Let's just put the baby gates up across the parlor and the

stairs," I decided. "But make sure all the food is put away. Nothing on the counters. We don't want another potato chip incident."

"I'll give her one of those chewy-bones," Madison volunteered. "That might keep her out of trouble."

It might keep her out of trouble for all of ten minutes. I didn't know what sort of testing the manufacturer of those bones did to warrant the "long-lasting" proclamation on their packaging, but Cagney went through one of those bones like she was the Tasmanian Devil in a Bugs Bunny cartoon. But they were safe, not a choking hazard, and were supposed to provide dental benefits, so giving her a bone wouldn't hurt.

"Taco needs a treat as well," Henry spoke up. "It's not fair for Cagney to get a bone and not give him something."

Taco was perfectly capable of stealing whatever he wanted from Cagney. The pup was still intimidated by the cat and would quickly relinquish her treat, watching in dismay as the cat ate her liver snacks or whatever. Having both of them in the house was a King Solomon level exercise in fairness.

"Taco can have his catnip toy," I told Henry. "And you can put that crinkle mat in the parlor for him."

Thankfully the baby gates were no barrier to Taco who deftly jumped right over them. I was surprised Cagney hadn't attempted the same, but she was wary of the gates. After knocking one over and hearing the clatter of it hitting the ground, she gave them a respectful distance. It meant Taco still had the run of the house, free to go wherever he wanted as well as get some much-needed peace from the energetic puppy, while Cagney could be restrained to areas of the house where she could do minimal damage.

Once more I gave thanks that Cagney's chewing phase hadn't led to her damaging the beautiful wood trim in the house or any of my furniture. If the dog kept her mischief to stealing potato chips and tossing cushions around the room, then I'd be happy.

We ate our donut-breakfast, got the cat and dog settled for the day, then all piled into the Judge's SUV to head to the VFW. As Judge Beck maneuvered the SUV into a parking space. I grimaced to see a group of about twenty people hovering outside the VFW doors.

"People are lined up outside," Henry commented. "I didn't think we were supposed to open until eight o'clock."

"Early birds," Madison told him with a knowing nod. "They show up at the crack of dawn hoping to grab stuff before it's all picked over."

"But it's a yard sale," Henry countered. "It's not like the five dollar TV for the first person in line on Black Friday. Most of the stuff we're selling is junk."

"Like you wouldn't be lined up to buy that giant witch," I teased him. "For some people, being the first to a yard sale is fun and exciting. Other people like to fix up and resell items in their online stores, so being able to get the best stuff before it's gone is part of their business."

Henry nodded. "I can see that. When I open my antique shop, I'll probably be going to yard sales and auctions, trying to find cool stuff that other people think is junk."

"Exactly." I unbuckled my seatbelt. "Now let's get in there. I have a feeling Matt is going to open early for these people so we need to be ready."

We went around the side of the building, ringing the bell at the heavy metal door that served as an emergency exit. Matt opened it, glancing quickly out before ushering us inside.

"Think we can open the doors in fifteen minutes?" he asked as we hurried down the corridor and into the huge room where all the tables were set up.

I quickly took in the scene. Daisy, Olive, Suzette, and Kat were already here as was Bert and two other men I didn't recognize. Daisy was already positioned behind one of the registers, counting cash and opening rolls of coins. Olive was making her way to the other one, a bulging bank bag in her hand.

The tables were neat and organized, just as we'd left them. Suzette and Kat were chatting next to the huge urns of coffee, cups, sweetener, and individual creamers ready to go. A can for donations sat next to one of the urns.

"We can open in fifteen," I told Matt. We'd position two people by the door to help guide people in, two people by the coffee station, and the rest of us helping customers and doing cleanup. Matt had six volunteers running food concessions since the money for that would go to the VFW in return for them letting us use the space.

A chime sounded from the side door. Matt waved at the judge. "Nate, can you stand by the front door? Let the customers know we're opening soon, but keep it locked."

Judge Beck nodded, heading off in that direction. I quickly made the rounds, letting the volunteers know the revised opening time. As I looped back, I saw Violet and Peony walking in.

My heart wrenched at the sight of the younger girl. She was thinner than when I'd last seen her. Her eyes darted around, never daring to land on anyone for more than a brief second. As I headed toward them, Peony's gaze landed on her feet, her shoulders hunched forward defensively. She wasn't the sassy and confident teen of last year, and that made me sad. I hoped that sometime soon, she'd feel comfortable once more in our town and regain some of her spark.

"Peony!"

The girl's head shot up at Madison's voice, her eyes

widening as Madison wrapped her arms around the other girl's shoulders in a huge hug.

"I'm so glad you're here! Come help me with the purses. You wouldn't believe the weird stuff people have donated. There's one purse that looks like a parrot. It's even got feathers. Come on." Madison grabbed Peony's hand and dragged the other girl away.

I bit back a smile at Peony's shocked expression, relieved to see the girl begin to relax with Madison's enthusiastic welcome and lively chatter. Madison was truly a wonderful person and a good friend. Peony might encounter some hostile looks and maybe even a few harsh words from people today, but I knew she'd get through it with Madison by her side.

Violet gave her sister a quick thumbs-up, then went over to one of the other tables. I made my way toward Judge Beck, who was still by the front door.

"You okay with that?" I asked, seeing that he was watching his daughter and Peony.

"I'm going to have to be okay with that," he said ruefully. "You're right. I have to put my faith in the system. And in my daughter. Honestly I'm proud of her helping Peony out like this. I trust that she'll do the right thing."

I nodded. "The 'right thing' is sticking by a friend who's been through some dark times. It's keeping boundaries between right and wrong, but also being kind enough to know when someone needs help. It's giving people a second chance."

The judge put his arm around my shoulder, snugging me close against his side. "People can change. Being in the legal profession, it's hard to remember that. I'm not that man I was in college, or even the man I was a year ago. People *do* grow and change."

"I'm not who I was in college either." I wrapped my arm

around his waist. "We're the sum of a lifetime of experiences. I hate to think that one bad choice isn't something a person can come back from. It might not be easy, but admitting you've done wrong and working hard to do right going forward should mean forgiveness and a second chance."

He kissed the top of my head. "Optimist."

"I like to keep my faith in humanity. Otherwise, everything feels so darned depressing."

"That's a philosophy I need to adopt," he told me.

"Let's open these doors!" Matt announced, clapping his hands for attention.

The judge grimaced. "Better stand back. I think stampede is going to be the operative word here."

I did as he said. Judge Beck opened the door and jumped out of the way before he could be trampled by the rush. The crowd of mostly middle-aged woman had grown to over three dozen in the fifteen minutes we'd been inside. Once over the threshold, they scattered, quickly eyeing the areas they wanted. Two of the women were practically in a race as they headed for the purses, picking up speed with each stride. I saw the alarmed expression on both Madison and Peony's faces, and headed over in case they needed help breaking up a fight over that parrot purse or something.

Surprisingly, the parrot purse was quickly snatched up, as were the handful of designer-brand purses. I watched the women make their way to the registers, sure that those items would be listed for sale online within the week.

I headed over to help Henry at the ties-and-scarves table, when a woman caught my sleeve.

"Excuse me. Are there any other holiday decorations?" she asked.

"Christmas stuff is over there." I pointed to the left where four tables loaded with knickknacks and ornaments were flanked by three Christmas trees. "Halloween is over there.

And the Easter, Fourth of July, and Thanksgiving stuff is over there."

"No. I mean, I know." She smiled. "I've already been through all of that. I wondered if you didn't have more stuff in a back room somewhere."

"Everything's out on the tables," I told her. It was a charity yard sale, after all. Our goal was to sell every last item before the end of the day. We wanted everything out the door as fast as possible. There would be no reason to hold extra stock in a back room and potentially miss out on the one person who may have wanted to buy it. I glanced at her shopping bag and saw Christmas nutcracker, a handful of ornaments and a small tablecloth.

"I really wanted some Halloween stuff," she went on. "I just bought a new house and really want to do it up this year."

Drat. Too bad we couldn't have sold her that six foot witch that was currently gracing my foyer.

"I'm sorry but everything we have is out on the tables," I repeated. "But see that teenage boy over there?" I pointed to Henry, who was holding up a leather tie, trying his best to sell it to a man old enough to be his grandfather. "If you're looking for something specific in terms of Halloween decorations, he's the one to ask."

She headed toward Henry, while I made the rounds, cleaning up the tables and helping customers looking for specific items. The morning flew by and by lunch I headed over to take over cashier duties from Daisy. Bert Peter had relieved Olive and was working by my side, ringing up the purchases of a steady stream of customers. By two o'clock, the rush had tapered off a bit and both Bert and I were able to catch our breaths. Matt brought us each a soda and we stood at the registers, watching customers browse and ringing up purchases at a much less frantic pace.

"Those early birds were crazy," Bert commented as he carefully wrapped a vase for a customer. "You know the funny thing was that I recognized some of my neighbors. A few of them were here for hours, carefully picking through each table of stuff like they were looking for buried treasure."

"For all we know some of this stuff could *be* buried treasure," I said only half teasing. "I had Henry glance over most of it since he knows more about antiques than the rest of us put together, but he's not an expert. For all we know, we may have sold a Rembrandt for three bucks."

"I hope not. We should at least get twenty dollars for a genuine Rembrandt," Bert joked. "Actually I got to laughing thinking of my neighbors here buying stuff and replacing what they'd just donated. Or maybe buying back what they had donated."

"Buying back what they weren't supposed to have donated and hoping their husband or wife didn't realize the golf clubs, or the favorite T-shirt, or the ugly vase was gone before they could return it?" I snorted, thinking that had been the plot of an episode in nearly every '80s sitcom.

"Exactly." Bert shook his head, grinning. "There were a few ugly vases in some of those boxes. And at least one set of golf clubs."

"One of the early birds grabbed the golf clubs the moment she was through the door," I remembered. "I think you're right, Bert."

"Her husband hasn't played in the last five years, and they were just taking up space in the garage, so she donated them. But then he came home that night and announced he'd joined a golfing team and their first game was next Saturday."

I laughed. "Panic! She had to buy those golf clubs back before he realized she'd gotten rid of them."

"Well, I hope she got here in time. And all those people buying back the ugly vases and old concert T-shirts as well."

"I know better than to give away old T-shirts. Judge Beck has some that are so threadbare you could read through them. They must be twenty years old. I think he'll go to his grave with those T-shirts."

"Are you making fun of my valuable collection of pub and concert T-shirts?" a voice said behind me.

"Guilty as charged, Your Honor." I leaned back to look up at Judge Beck. His arms came around me and my heart raced at the public display of affection.

"I'm hoping whoever donated Sandy wasn't here, frantically trying to buy her back," he commented.

"Given that Sandy was probably lifted off a golf course in South Carolina, too bad." I smiled at him. "She'll just have to explain to her husband that Sandy has been lost forever."

"Sandy?" Bert asked with a frown.

"A sand wedge I took the liberty of buying pre-sale," the judge told him. "It's a perk of having hundreds of boxes in the house for the last two weeks. I get early dibs on a nice golf club."

"A nice golf club that was probably yours originally," I teased.

Bert laughed. "Guess I'm lucky. There's nothing here that I'm particularly interested in bringing home with me. I think it's because I've spent the last year going through my uncle's junk. I'm becoming one of those minimalist people."

"You wouldn't be saying that if you'd accidentally given away your spouse's T-shirt collection, or golf clubs," I told him.

"Good thing I don't have a spouse," he replied.

"All this talk about giving away T-shirts." Judge Beck shuddered. "I think I'm going to have to install locks on my dresser drawers. Especially after the attempted robbery last night."

"You had a robbery last night?" Bert's eyes widened.

I rolled my eyes. "Some kids broke into my old garage and tossed it. Nothing was stolen. There was no real damage. But because the judge is the judge, we're going to be installing some sort of Fort Knox level security system in the next week."

"I've been thinking about doing the same," Bert confessed. "Someone broke into my car Thursday night. Popped open the trunk and made a mess. They tried to get into my garage, but didn't do anything except break the locked handle."

"I'm starting to lose my faith in humanity," Judge Beck told me. "You might be an optimist, but my positive vibes are slipping."

"Your positive vibes slipped a long time ago." I turned to Bert. "I'm so sorry your car was vandalized. Did you report it to the police? I was reluctant to do so, but now I'm kind of glad I did if there is a group of kids going around breaking into garages and cars."

"I doubt it's the same group of kids in our neighborhood and in Bert's," the judge pointed out.

"Maybe not, but it's clearly a trend," I told him. "It could be some TikTok challenge or something. Kids do weird things nowadays."

Ugh, I sounded like such an old fogy. Soon I'd be rocking on my porch, drinking prune juice, and yelling at everyone to get off my lawn.

"No one else in our neighborhood had a break in," Bert said. "Although the Winfords four doors down said someone knocked over their garbage cans. It was probably just some kids causing trouble."

"I don't think anyone else in our neighborhood was robbed either," I told him. "I figured the kids got scared after tossing our garage, or got spooked by a passing car or a barking dog and decided to hightail it out of there."

"Probably the same with me," Bert said. "A few people on our block work late shifts, and we're all super aware of strange cars or people wandering around in the middle of the night. Either way, I'm going to start parking my car in my garage at night, just to be safe."

"And we're putting in a security system with cameras and alarms. And an electronic opener on the garage," the judge told him. "I don't like the idea of someone being right outside the house and going through the garage—not with my kids and Kay inside."

"I'm less concerned, but am going along with this security stuff to keep the peace," I told Bert, holding back a smile.

"I might be a single-guy, but keeping the peace sounds like a good plan." Bert turned to the judge. "And text me with your recommendations on cameras and alarms. I always thought I lived in a safe neighborhood, but maybe over the years it's gotten less safe. Either way, I'd rather this not happen again or end up with my house being robbed or something. Better to take precautions and not need them then be ill prepared."

As much as I felt the whole security system thing was overkill, I kind of agreed. Maybe it was a good thing to have cameras and security systems, just in case.

And hopefully we'd never need them.

CHAPTER 10

"*M*rs. Carrera?"

The woman walking across the lobby on three inch heels was absolutely not what I expected when I thought of a forensic anthropologist. Rachel Basava was petite, half my age, and just as elegant as her fashionable stilettos. Her hair hung down past her waist in a glossy, ebony waterfall. Her makeup was subtle and flattering. The hand she held out had beautifully manicured nails. The only thing stereotypical about her was the oversized black-framed glasses and the white lab coat over her smart navy blue pantsuit.

"Yes. I'm Kay Carrera. Thank you so much for meeting with me, Doctor Basava."

"Please, call me Rachel." She laughed as she shook my hand. "I can tell from your expression you were expecting someone who looked like they'd just come from a dig. Most of my work is done in an office or a lab, but if it makes you feel any better, I don't wear these shoes in the field. Or this suit."

"Sorry." I grimaced at my lack of manners. "I'll admit I

was expecting a female Indiana Jones or that woman from the *Bones* show on television."

"Not Rachel Weisz from *The Mummy?*" she teased.

"Now *that* I can see." I took a step back and nodded. "Absolutely. All you need is Brendan Fraser."

"Well, I'm packed and ready to travel to Egypt with Brendan Fraser any day, any time." She motioned toward the box at my feet. "Let's take these into my office and we'll see what you've got here."

I picked up the box and followed her across the lobby, down a hallway, and into a tiny office. Boxes lined the walls, and papers were in precariously tall stacks everywhere. Books were on the two chairs opposite the desk. Rachel grabbed the books from one chair while I set the box on her desk.

I opened the box and went to take one of the bones out, only to hesitate when I saw Rachel donning a pair of gloves.

"Oh no! I didn't even think about that. I've touched all of these with my bare hands, and I'm pretty sure a few of the others who were sorting through the donations have as well."

She waved a blue gloved hand. "Don't worry. These things happen. I've had bones turned up during excavation that well-meaning people gathered up to keep safe. You're not the first. Plus, I'm sure whoever donated them also touched them, and possibly generations before them. There's a possibility these bones were for medical use, which means hundreds of hands have touched them. I'm just gloving up as a precaution."

That made me feel a bit better, but I still stood back and let her remove them from the box rather than add to the prints and oils I'd already put on the items. As a private investigator, I should have known better. I should have put on gloves the moment I suspected the bones were real, but I wasn't used to dealing with potential crime scene evidence in a box of donated holiday decorations.

"Do you get a lot of that?" I asked her. "Bones turned up during excavation, I mean?"

Rachel carefully pulled a foot from the box, turning it over in her hands. "That's the majority of the work I get from law enforcement and the M.E.'s office. Most of the time, they're from an old private cemetery that wasn't recorded. Farms get sold to development, and suddenly the family graveyard is unearthed. If the location was noted in the deed or the county record, then the developer lets us know. We go out to scan the area, find the graves, and work with the developer to notify descendants and relocate the bodies. Sadly, the smaller cemeteries often get lost and forgotten, and there have been a few surprises when someone goes to dig a foundation for a house."

"My friend Miles—he's a county deputy—was saying that. He told me there was a case in a neighboring county where a developer accidently excavated a family graveyard." I thought about Suzette's property and some of the developments around where we lived, and wondered if the developer who'd put in our houses had needed to relocate graves. "How long does it take? To find and move the bodies, that is."

"Months. Sometimes more." She set the foot aside and pulled another bone from the box. "Drives the developers bonkers. They can't do anything on the area we cordon off until we're done. And we can't relocate bodies until we've made every effort to find out who the deceased were and try to contact their descendants. Eventually we *do* have to move the bodies, and just keep track of who is where in case someone turns up months later wanting to know what happened to great-great-great-aunt Mary's remains."

"And that's a full-time job?" I asked, wondering how

many unexpected private cemeteries were unearthed in the state each year.

"Heavens no." She set the bone aside and selected another. "I consult with law enforcement on bodies that are found where crime is suspected. I also work with museums in cataloging and writing articles about their displays. Basically there are crime-scene bones, bones accidently unearthed from a private cemetery, ancient archeological bones donated to museums, spiritual bones that have been carved and are used in a religious context, and medical osteology."

"Medical osteology? Is that the bones that were donated to medical universities for student use and study?" I asked, thinking of the internet research Henry had done a few nights ago.

"Yes." She picked the foot back up and showed it to me. "See the wires? That's a dead giveaway, although this particular foot is a plaster reproduction. Bones that were prepared for use in medical studies often have springs, clasps, and wires. Occasionally they'll have specific sections cut away to display inner structures or even markings to show where muscles or nerves would be."

I peered into the box. "Other than the foot, none of the others has any of that."

She nodded. "They're not always modified that way. Sometimes you can tell by the way the bone is cleaned. The preparation leaves the bones white, and pristine, with pretty much no DNA remaining."

"So with a skeleton that was donated for medical use, you can't tell who it belonged to? What if the university program shuts down, or someone finds their great uncle's medical school skeleton in the attic, and wants to return it to the family?"

"There's no way of doing that," she explained. "When the bodies are donated, they are stripped of any identifying information, and only sometimes numbered. It was for privacy as well as ethical reasons. There is no way to identify them and return them to their family. Companies acted as middlemen between those purchasing the bones and the donors, and most of them never even marked the bones. With no DNA and no identifying numbers, there really is no way to trace those bones back to their families."

She continued to take bones out of the box, examine them, then set them aside as we spoke.

"So if any of these are medical bones, what do I do?" I asked. "Bury them?"

She chuckled. "Uh, no. That's against the law. It sounds ridiculous that you can't bury a donated skull in your back-yard, while you can keep it in a box in your attic. But you have to think about these things long-term. It would be considered an unregulated burial, and would cause problems if decades later someone bought your house and turned the skull up while putting in a vegetable garden."

I winced. "I can see that. The police would be called, the skull would be sent to the M.E.'s office. You'd end up having to look at it all over again. And the poor homeowner would probably freak out thinking their house had been the scene of a murder."

"Exactly." She turned a smaller bone over in her hands and put it aside. "You could have them cremated, but it would be at your own expense. See? That's why so many of these bones end up in a box in the attic."

"My friend's son found a website that buys and sells medical bones. Is that even legal?" I asked, not at all enthused that I might end up with a skull in my attic—at least until I could manage to pawn it off on some unsuspecting neighbor collecting for a charity yard sale, which I was beginning to think was what had happened to me.

"Yes, it absolutely is legal, although you'll want to make

sure it's a reputable company who checks the bones just as I'm doing now. Those bones usually are sold to museums, or back into the medical university market, or to private collectors. I have a friend who is a dental osteology enthusiast. He's a dentist, and he's fascinated by the interesting specimens used in teaching through the centuries."

As hobbies went, that sounded pretty weird.

"It's fascinating, actually." Rachel went on. "In the 1920s medical and dental schools required students to have their own skeleton or skull for their studies. At the turn of the nineteenth century, there weren't enough donated bodies for the anatomy classes or for each student to purchase their own skeleton, so grave robbing was a problem. Companies sprang up that purchased bodies from overseas to satisfy the need."

"*Purchased?*" My mouth dropped open. "That's horrible. I thought they were donated for medical use, like we do with organ donation nowadays."

"Some were, but with demand outstripping supply, these companies were willing to pay." She shot me a quick smile. "Not every culture has the same rituals and beliefs concerning the dead and bodies as we have here in the U.S. Plus if you're poor and desperate, and your uncle just passed away, it's difficult to turn down an offer that might put food on your table and save you the cost of burial. It sounds horrible, but lots of people still make that decision based on the high cost of funerals and interment or cremation today. It's illegal to sell recent human remains even ones that are donated, for ethical reasons, but if you don't have thousands of dollars for a cremation, an option is to donate your loved one's body to science. For the minimal cost of shipping, any unused remains are cremated and sent back to the family."

I had no idea. Eli and I had thankfully prepaid for our funerals and grave plots decades ago, spurred on to take care of our arrangements ahead of time after going through the burial of both of our parents. I was grateful that all I'd needed to do was sign a few papers and grieve when Eli had passed, but looking back, I remembered how we'd spent nearly thirty thousand dollars in prepayments for both of us. Fifteen thousand dollars each. I couldn't imagine being faced with that bill in the financial circumstances I'd been in at the time Eli had died.

"Nowadays donated bodies are kept at the research facility or museum and never transferred to the public," Rachel said. "If a museum or a facility closes, the remains are then cremated and returned to the family, or they are transferred to whatever research facility takes over their projects and/or collections."

"So if any of these are real," I motioned to the bones Rachel had placed on the desk, "then they're a hundred years old? Because currently donated remains wouldn't have ended up in private hands, right? Do you need to carbon date them or something to tell?"

"Although most medical bones are from the '20s, bones were being sold into private hands for medical study up until 1985 when India banned their sale, and skeletons coming from China weren't always suitable or sufficient. Plus by that time plastic and plaster reproductions were realistic enough that the need for actual remains had dropped significantly."

My grandmother had died in 1982. It was gruesome to think that she or one of her friends could be bones in someone's attic. Although from what Rachel had said, it was more likely they would have been in a university than purchased by a medical student at that point in time.

I watched as Rachel continued to examine each bone, putting them in distinct parts of her desk. By the time the box was empty, she had three piles of bones.

"These are plaster." She smiled at me. "And they're nicely

done. Someone will really enjoy putting these out for Halloween."

"That's good to know." I eyed the other two piles anxiously.

"These are resin." She held her hand over a second pile, then moved to the third pile. "This is an actual bone."

I had a bad feeling in the pit of my stomach. "So, the skull is a medical bone? We're okay to donate it somewhere?"

"No." Her expression was somber as she picked up the skull. "Remember I said that medical bones were meticulously cleaned? That there was nothing there as far as DNA? This skull has staining that's consistent with natural decomposition. It's been cleaned, but not professionally."

"So it was turned up in an accidental excavation?" I asked, not sure if that was a better scenario than the other one running through my mind. "A farmer turned it up when plowing a field that used to be a private cemetery, and rather than contact the authorities, he just kept it in his attic?"

She shook her head. "There are certain things about this skull that make me believe it was not buried in anything deeper than a shallow grave. Although I need to do more testing, I'd judge this skull was from a woman who died about five years ago. The question I have is why she went from what I assume was a shallow grave to a box of donated Halloween decorations."

That was a question I had as well, but as Rachel spoke, I could only focus on one thing.

"Murder?"

"Murder," Rachel confirmed. "Or at the very least, improper disposal of a body. I'm thinking murder as this is not the skull of an elderly woman."

I stared in horror at the skull. A woman. Five-ish years ago a woman had been killed, and for the last few days I'd been carrying her bones around in a box. What if the box with the skull had never been donated? What if I'd just assumed it was fake and had sold it at the yard sale? A woman had died, and this might have never come to light, her skull forever remaining in a box in someone's attic.

Clearly the murderer hadn't knowingly donated it. Someone else had. I thought back on my joking conversation with Bert Peter at the yard sale, laughing over the idea that a wife would be lined up outside to rush in and buy back her husband's golf clubs before he realized she'd given them away.

Was this the same scenario, only with a skull—with the skull of someone who'd been murdered? Had a husband or wife been going through the attic, boxed up what they thought were Halloween decorations and given them away? Had the murderer discovered what had happened? Did they show up at the yard sale, looking for the bones in the hopes of buying them back before anyone realized what they were?

My mind raced through all the customers we'd had, all the decorations we'd sold. At least five people had inquired specifically about Halloween decorations to me, and I was sure other volunteers had gotten questions as well. Along with the Christmas ornaments, Halloween decorations were among the most popular of the items we'd sold on Sunday.

As Rachel dialed the police, I stared at the skull wondering who the victim had been and how in the world I could possibly figure out who had donated the skull. While I thought, a shadow materialized in the corner of the room, passing through Rachel as it floated over to the desk.

The other woman shivered, looking around for the sudden draft as she spoke to the police. I suddenly realized this was the same shadow that had appeared in my house, the one who had been rolling the apple out of the fruit basket. I hadn't wanted to believe the ghost was connected to the skull. Spirits imprinted themselves on all sorts of items and my house had been full of items for the yard sale.

But this ghost wasn't here because an old scarf or alarm clock or book had been important in their life or death, this ghost was here because the skull was hers.

Hers. She'd been young when she'd been murdered. I couldn't tell her exact age at the time of death from the ghost hovering over the desk, but I got the feeling she'd been nineteen or twenty. Had she hovered around her skull ever since her death? Where was the rest of her body? And how had the skull of a murdered woman ended up in a box of donated Halloween decorations? Was the donor the murderer? Or had they somehow acquired the skull as I had and displayed it each Halloween, thinking it was fake?

As the spirit reached out a ghostly hand to the skull, I knew then that, as usual, I couldn't just let the police handle this case. I'd been one of the main volunteers when it came to the charity yard sale. I'd been the one who'd stored all the donations in my house and garage. I'd been the one who'd accepted every box of items.

If anyone had a chance of figuring out where the skull came from, it was me. And finding out where the skull came from was most likely the key in finding out who murdered this young woman.

CHAPTER 11

A uniformed officer with the Milford police arrived first, followed by my nemesis, Detective Keeler.

He scowled at me. "Figures. I should have known it was you. If there's a murder, or a body, then I can bet on it that you'll have your nose right in the middle of the investigation."

We had a less-than-friendly history, but his accusation was really unfair. He wouldn't even have this piece of evidence if my friends and I hadn't noticed there was something very realistic about some of the Halloween decorations.

"Oh, relax Desmond." Rachel scolded, clearly on better terms with the detective than I was. "She thought it was just a realistic replica, or possibly a skull from a medical college program. It's not like she suspected murder."

But I *had* suspected murder. The ghost that had appeared in my house Thursday night had been a tip-off, but it's not like I wanted to admit that to anyone.

"And it's definitely murder?" Keeler asked the anthropologist.

"I can't prove cause of death just from the skull, but I can tell that this was a woman between the ages of seventeen and twenty-five when she died." Rachel turned the skull and pointed to the back molars. "The wisdom teeth hadn't come in, but based on their position I'd guess she was around twenty. Judging from the staining and the condition of the bone, I'd say she died roughly five years ago. I don't know of any reason for someone to have a skull from a death five years ago without some sort of foul play being involved."

"You don't think it might have been turned up by a farmer, or someone excavating? Like that case a few years back over in Halfort County?" Keeler asked.

She shook her head. "No, those sort of bones would be very obviously old. Someone who died five years ago would have been buried in a cemetery with a sealed casket and a grave liner or a vault. No one accidently turns those bodies up while digging for a foundation."

The detective sighed. "Woman? Early twenties and died about five years ago? How sure are you of that?"

"Pretty sure." Rachel picked the skull up once more, turning it over in her gloved hands. "I'll know more once I get this into my lab, but if I were you, I'd be looking at missing person's reports in the last ten years for women under the age of twenty five. Nothing recent, though. This skull was in the ground for at least a few years."

Keller nodded. "Do you think there's any DNA we can get from this?"

"Yes. And even if there's not a DNA match to anything you have on record, I should at least be able to tell you more about her."

"That would help," Keeler said. "She may have been from out of state. Her killer might have transported her bones here after her death. Anything we can get to narrow down who she was would help."

He handed over an evidence bag and Rachel carefully put the skull inside. "I'll coordinate with your medical examiner and cc you on my e-mails. I'm assuming you'll take the lead in this?"

"Right now I'm it. There's another detective, but I'll only bring him in as needed," Keeler replied.

I grimaced, hoping that he didn't bring Detective Toots into the case. The man was a horrible investigator and a worse cop. He needed to be in another line of work, but until then we were stuck with him. Hopefully the county sheriff's department could keep him busy with cold cases and administrative stuff until they could get him reassigned elsewhere.

"And now I need to hear how you managed to come across the skull," Keeler said, turning to me.

I told him about the charity yard sale and the boxes of donations that had been stacked everywhere in my house. "It looked so real," I told him. "Olive knew someone who put her in touch with Doctor Basava, and she was gracious enough to make room in her schedule today for me. I was hoping it was fake, or that it had been purchased by a medical student and sat in someone's attic for decades."

Detective Keeler fixed me with a hard stare. "Please tell me you tracked who gave what, perhaps so you could issue receipts for tax reasons?"

I flushed. "No. We issued blank donations receipts so people could fill in the items themselves. Most of my staff were soliciting donations, and just dropping the boxes off at my house to be sorted and priced later. We're all volunteers. Nobody had the time to go through each box at the time of donation and catalogue the items."

"Is there at least a list of everyone who donated?" He asked.

"No, but I can ask everyone involved to put together a list. I can't guarantee it will be one hundred percent accurate, but

I think people will remember most of the houses and businesses that donated."

I was beginning to feel really inept at this whole charity organization thing.

Keeler sighed. "Any idea which box held the skull? As well as what other items were in the box with it?"

I nodded. "It was with a whole lot of other Halloween decorations, Christmas decorations, and a handful of Easter and Thanksgiving stuff."

"Who was the person who unpacked it?" the detective asked.

"It was Henry, Judge Beck's son." I'll admit I took a bit of glee in the fact that the detective stiffened at the name. I'd never fully appreciated the power that came with a judge-ship. Judge Beck was a fair and thoughtful man, but he was also firm when it came to the rule of law. In the courtroom he had a powerful presence that was downright terrifying. I'd seen him exert that same influence on occasion outside of the courtroom and it made me grateful that I hadn't been on the other side of that steely glare.

Now that we were dating and I was sure of his affection and regard, I found the whole thing a bit of a turn on, but in the beginning, I'd been so intimidated that I couldn't bring myself to call Judge Beck by his first name, even to myself.

Who was I kidding? I *still* didn't call him by his first name. And it was kind of funny that he wasn't even aware of it.

"*Judge Beck's* son?"

I'll give Detective Keeler credit, his voice didn't even waver as he clarified the fact with me.

"Yes. He's with his mother this week."

I could see the wheels turning in the detective's brain. "I'll still need to clear it through the judge before I go talk to the boy," he mused.

"I'm sure the judge would want to be present at the time of your questioning as well," I pointed out.

Keeler nodded. "Of course. Is anything left from that box? The box itself? Anything that might spur the boy's memory of everything that was in it?"

"Most of the boxes were broken down for recycling after the event," I told him. "I wouldn't be able to tell what the original was from the few that are left. And while there are some items leftover from the yard sale in my garage, I wouldn't know what was in that particular box. I was sorting through other donations at the time."

"I'll need to go through the remaining yard sale items," he told me. "So please don't dispose of anything at this time."

I nodded, thinking that the neat stack of boxes in my garage was about to become very un-neat.

CHAPTER 12

J texted Judge Beck on my way in to work, wanting to give him a heads-up in case Detective Keeler contacted him today. He called me right away, getting the details as well as assurances that I was okay.

Newsflash—I wasn't okay.

"She was in her early twenties," I told the judge, my vision misting at the thought. "Around the same age as Violet and Molly. I'm struggling with the thought that a young woman lost her life roughly five years ago and that her skull and maybe the rest of her remains were in someone's basement or attic in a box. A box!"

It was so horrifying. I kept thinking of my young friends, of Madison, of all the teens Daisy worked with. They all deserved to live until a ripe old age, not die so young and end up missing, fate unknown, all while their skull was in a box of cheap decorations. Murder was always a horrible crime, but this murder felt particularly heinous.

"The crimes against children always hit me the hardest," the judge replied. "And while early twenties might not be a child in the eyes of the law, it's someone who lost their life far too early."

I nodded, even though he couldn't see the motion, thinking suddenly of Holt Dupree. He'd been twenty-two. And that had been part of what had been so tragic about his death. A young man with a promising future had died—not that a promising future should be the only factor in calculating his loss. He'd died too young. And the younger girl who'd unintentionally caused his death would pay for it the rest of her life, even though her prison time was over. Two lives ruined by a reckless stupid decision made in greed.

What had happened with this girl whose skull had ended up in a box of donated items? Like Holt, had she died unintentionally? Had her killer panicked when the drug he gave her resulted in her death? Unlike Peony, had this girl's killer not come forward with their crime, instead hiding the body and hoping it was never found? Or had she been murdered in cold blood by some psychotic individual? By a jealous boyfriend? In a robbery? Or to hide a sexual assault?

I wanted answers just as much as Detective Keeler did.

Promising we'd talk more tonight, I hung up with the judge and pulled into the parking lot at work.

Inside, I again went over what the forensic anthropologist had said, and my conversation with the detective.

"So I guess you want all of us to make a list of where we picked up donations, the size and number of the boxes, and any items we knew were in them?" Molly asked, grabbing a notepad in anticipation of the assignment.

"Everything you can remember," I told her before turning to J.T. with an apologetic smile. "You too, please."

"It's a short list." He grimaced. "Clearly I'm not cut out for this soliciting-for-donations thing. I got a couple of boxes of books from one neighbor and a handful of ties from the other. I told Matt I'd make up for my shortcomings with a cash donation."

In the world of non-profit organizations, cash donations were more than welcome. But I told J.T. I'd still needed that list, just to satisfy Detective Keeler.

"Should I comment on these?" Molly asked, scribbling on the notepad. "I'll admit that I peeked at every single box I picked up because I'm nosy, and because I was checking to see if there was anything I might like to buy. Hunter's and my décor right now would be best labeled poverty-chic. I'm not ashamed to admit I bought a few of those curtains and some mismatched flatware from the yard sale."

"There's no shame in that," I told the girl. "In my first apartment, my dresser came from the curb on bulk-trash day. I felt like a thief pulling up in the middle of the night and shoving it into the back of my Honda. I had to tie the hatch down because it wouldn't close. The whole way home I was worried I'd be arrested."

I still wasn't completely sure taking stuff off the curb on garbage night was totally legal. Given how many people scarfed up items from the curb during rental evictions, I assumed if it wasn't legal, the cops turned a blind eye to the activity.

"It's actually kind of fun, haunting yard sales and thrift stores for bargains," Molly said. "I've picked up most of my kitchenware from Secondhand Treasures—the bargain store run by St. Peter's Church. It's crazy how people donate stuff that's practically brand new and in the box. I'm not sure my blender was even used."

"Well, here's my list." J.T. handed me a sheet of paper with contact information for two of his neighbors. "And I'm totally supportive of you working this case, Kay. Just make sure you keep me in the loop on everything. It's going to make a great episode for my YouTube channel."

"It might take a while before this mystery is solved," I warned him. "First we need to figure out where the skull came from, then if the people who donated it were even aware it was real. For all we know, they may have bought those decorations at another yard sale."

"I doubt it," Molly said. "I mean, there's realistic, and there's real. I can't imagine someone picked that skull up and didn't at least wonder. You said Henry suspected right away, and so did your neighbor Kat. Plus, if they're innocent, then they must have acquired it fairly recently. You said five years, right? Given time for decomposition, they had to have gotten the skull in the last year or two at most."

I nodded. "True. I just don't want to immediately assume we've got a Norman Bates living nearby with a body in the attic. I came into possession of the skull through innocent means, and I'd want to extend someone else that same presumption of innocence."

"Understand. But you *know* this has to be Carly Billings's skull, right?" Molly waved her pen at me. "It *has* to be. It's the only cold missing-persons case in the county. She vanished five years ago. She was twenty. We were just talking about her Friday. This can't be a coincidence."

"Yes, it can be a coincidence," I pointed out. "I agree that there's a good chance the skull is Carly's, but it might also be any number of young women who have gone missing from neighboring states, or even farther away. She could have been passing through the area when she was murdered."

"It's Carly. I just know it," Molly said, her voice determined. "Finally her family and friends will have some closure, and she'll be able to rest in peace. Finally her killer will be brought to justice."

I remembered the ghost in my kitchen, the apple rolling across the counter. Would Carly's spirit stay with the skull? Or would she continue to lurk around my house, or me? In the past, some ghosts had latched onto me, either realizing I could see them or because they had some idea that I might be able to help them. I did want to help Carly, but there was only so much I could do.

And I wasn't positive the ghost *was* Carly.

"Dr. Basava is doing tests in the lab," I told J.T. and Molly. "She'll coordinate with the Medical Examiner's office with the results, but she's hopeful that there will be enough DNA to match to a missing person's report. Until then, the focus is on figuring out where the skull came from."

"All the more reason for you to help Detective Keeler," Molly said. "You helped put together this fundraiser. The boxes were all dropped off at your house. There are going to be a dozen lists, each with dozens of names and addresses on them. They'll all need to be checked out, and Keeler is only one guy."

"He can always enlist help from the uniforms," I pointed out.

"We're not a huge county. There are only so many deputies, and they have their own duties." Molly ticked the thoughts off on her fingers. "Toots is a waste of time. And although Keeler might be able to get some of the Milford officers to help, they're busy as well. He needs us."

I hid a smile. "Us?"

"Us." She motioned back and forth between herself and me. "I've gotten pretty good at this whole skip tracing thing. I can run backgrounds on suspects, dig into their social media. We'll solve the crime, find the killer, and J.T. will have an awesome episode to air on his channel."

"Molly can be in the video," J.T. said. "And you too, Kay."

"I'm not going to be in any more videos," I protested before turning to Molly. "But I do want your help on this. Everything we find needs to be turned over to Detective Keeler, though. I don't want to get on that man's bad side—

well, any more on his bad side than I already am. And we need to make sure we don't get behind on the work that's actually giving us a paycheck. Okay?"

"Okay." Molly grinned and spun back around to her computer. "Hang in there Carly Billings, or whoever you are. We're going to find out what happened to you, and we'll make sure your killer goes to jail."

CHAPTER 13

J was surprised to see Judge Beck's SUV in the driveway as I pulled in. When the kids were at Heather's he tended to work late, trying to catch up from what he'd missed the week he had Madison and Henry.

Taco made a quick escape between my legs as soon as I opened the door, eagerly anticipating his brief outdoor-time before dinner. Thankfully I managed to grab Cagney by the collar before she could race off after the cat. I was used to coming home first and having her confined either in her crate or barricaded in the parlor with baby gates.

"Has Cagney been out?" I called to Judge Beck.

"I let her in the backyard to relieve herself, but she hasn't been for her evening walk yet," he called back.

When Madison and Henry were here, they took turns taking Cagney for a quick walk right when they got home, then a later one after dinner. When it was just the judge and me, we tended to forgo the earlier walk in favor of letting the pup run around the backyard for a bit.

Promising Cagney more exercise after dinner, I plopped my bag on a chair and headed into the kitchen. The judge was setting out four large pizza boxes on the island next to a stack of plates and napkins.

"Feeling especially hungry tonight?" I teased. Carryout wasn't an uncommon dinner choice, although we tried to cook more nutritious meals when the kids were here.

"Yes, but not four-large-pizzas hungry. Heather is bringing the kids over in a few minutes. Detective Keeler wants to interview Henry about the skull, and we thought it would be easier for him to remember details if he were in the same place as when he'd unboxed it."

"It's a good idea. Why don't I grab some of the boxes we broke down for recycling and tape them back up so we can use them as props," I suggested.

I went out to the garage and brought a few of the empty boxes in, quickly taping them back together and stacking them in the foyer. On my last trip back from the garage Taco met me at the back door, ready to come in for his dinner.

He glanced down at the diet kibble as I poured it into his bowl, then sent me a disgusted look.

"Okay. Okay." I picked up the bowl, added some of his usual Happy Cat food and mixed them together. The cat's mood improved the moment I pulled the familiar bag out from the cabinet, and he went into a frenzy of meows and circles, darting in front of me until I set the food down.

He stared at the contents for a few seconds, then carefully ate one piece of kibble.

"If you're going to be picky, then you're going to bed hungry tonight," I told him. "Half of your dinner is the diet stuff, so it's gonna be a lean meal if all you eat is the Happy Cat food."

He ignored me, pawing at his food, and carefully selecting certain morsels. I decided not to stress over my cat's dinner, and instead got Cagney's food together.

The pup was in the foyer, staring at the six-foot tall witch that Henry had positioned in the corner of the room. He hadn't managed to take it upstairs before he'd left for Heather's and I didn't mind as long as it was out of the way. Cagney did seem to mind. She hadn't noticed the witch when the room had been filled with boxes, but when we'd hauled them all to the VFW on Sunday, she'd gotten a good look at the thing and was definitely having mixed feelings about the decoration.

I'd joked with Daisy about her potentially chewing it up, but Cagney didn't want to get within three feet of the witch. She eyed it suspiciously each time she passed, giving it a wide berth and keeping it in view until she was safely in another room. Hopefully she'd get used to it soon.

"Cagney! Dinner!"

The pup gave the witch one more glance, a low growl coming from her throat. Then she raced over to me and shoved her head into her food bowl, making sure she was positioned to keep the witch in view as she ate.

"It's not going to hurt you, silly girl," I scolded. Still, I wondered whether having the witch in the foyer was a good idea after all. Next week when Henry came back, I might need to urge him to find space in his room for the witch, otherwise it might need to go into the garage with the left-over yard sale stuff, gardening tools, and bags of ice melt.

There was a knock at the door that sent Cagney into a frenzy of barking, puppy kibble raining from her jowls as she ran across the foyer. I held her back by her collar and ushered Heather and the kids inside.

"There's pizza in the kitchen," I told them. "Go ahead and eat before the detective gets here."

The kids raced for the food, while Heather bent down to greet Cagney. The pup squirmed, licking her face and whining. It made me a little sad that things hadn't worked out for Heather and the puppy. Although I was thrilled to have

Cagney here with the judge and me, I could tell that Heather missed the dog, and that Cagney had developed quite an affection for the woman who'd temporarily adopted her.

The judge came down the stairs, pausing halfway as he saw his ex-wife with his dog. He'd changed into a pair of sweatpants and one of his ancient T-shirts, and in my opinion looked just as good as he did in his suit.

Heather looked up at him, still kneeling with Cagney dancing around her. For a brief second their eyes met, and I felt a stab of jealousy.

Of course he still had feelings for her. They had almost twenty years of history between them. She was the mother of his children. There would always be a place in his heart for her, and I'd be a hypocrite if I let it bother me. I still loved Eli. I'd always love Eli. But there was room in our hearts for so much more than one person.

It was over between the judge and Heather. Over. The feelings he had for her would never be what they were. And Judge Beck was an honest, honorable man. If that ever changed, he'd tell me. So I shoved the little green-eyed monster away and let myself trust.

The judge continued descending the stairs, glancing toward the kitchen where his kids were loudly debating pizza toppings. Heather bent her head to give Cagney a quick kiss before standing and smiling over at me.

"Thanks for getting pizza for everyone," she said.

"Oh, it wasn't me. Judge Beck sprang for dinner." I motioned toward him.

He shot me a puzzled look, and I realized that I'd used his formal name—to his ex-wife who he clearly would be on an informal basis with. Trying to ignore the whole thing, I followed Heather into the kitchen, telling her about Cagney's latest antics. The judge came in after us, not mentioning the "weird formality" thing I had going on with him. We ate pizza, drank iced tea, and were just putting away the left-overs when Detective Keeler arrived.

The detective declined our offer of pizza, so we all gathered in the foyer to get started.

I handed Keeler a folder that held a packet of printouts. "I don't have everyone's lists yet, but this is five of them. At the top is the volunteer's name and contact information, then their list of who they remember getting donations from, along with anything they can recall about the boxes—sizes, how many, identifying marks, approximate weight, as well as if they recall anything that was in them. I'll text or e-mail the rest to you as I get them."

"Very thorough," he commented, making me a bit flustered at the unexpected compliment. Then he opened the folder and sighed, clearly disheartened by the amount of work ahead of him.

I winced in sympathy, knowing that Detective Toots wouldn't be much help with this. Actually, he'd probably be a significant hindrance.

"Okay." He closed the folder and looked at Henry. "Would it be easier if everyone tried to recreate Friday night when you found the skull?"

"Yes." The boy fidgeted nervously, glancing over at his father.

"Just tell the detective everything you remember," the judge told his son in a soothing voice. "Any little detail matters—like what other things were in the box, or what they were wrapped in."

Henry nodded. Judge Beck and I moved to stand where we remembered being on Friday night. Madison did the same. Keeler placed himself off to the side, recording device in hand, while Heather remained in the doorway to the kitchen, sipping her iced tea.

"It was a big box." Henry looked at the ones I'd taped

together as props. "Maybe about this size, only not quite as tall. I think the box came up to here."

"Roughly sixteen by eighteen," Keller commented as he wrote. "Approximately twelve inches deep."

Henry frowned in concentration. "There were Christmas ornaments on top, wrapped in tissue paper. Four of them were glass ornaments in boxes. Kat had been going through the box first, and I noticed she was really careful with those. They were in little boxes. She left them in their boxes, and put the ornaments over in a box by the dining room table. That's where we were putting the Christmas stuff since there was so much of it."

"Do you remember what any of the ornaments looked like?" Keeler asked.

"The wrapped ones were just ball ornaments, but the glass ones in the boxes were kind of cool. One was a type-writer. I thought the person who'd originally owned it might have been a writer or some sort of admin person, and that they'd gotten it as a gift. The other three were animals. I think a cat, a rabbit, and a mouse, but I'm not positive. I remember the typewriter, though."

"I'll text Kat since she was originally going through the box," I said, feeling a little guilty for not thinking of that before.

Keeler nodded, motioning for Henry to go on.

"There were some other decorations in the box—Easter, Saint Paddy's Day, Thanksgiving. I didn't pay much attention to them. Then under that were some Halloween things. I remember them because I love Halloween stuff. Dad let me keep the witch here by the staircase. Isn't it cool?"

"Cool enough to give me a heart attack every time I come down the stairs in the morning," Madison drawled.

"I'm just glad it's in your house and not in mine," Heather commented.

"What was the Halloween stuff in the box, Henry," Judge Beck gently urged before we all were derailed by the giant witch in my foyer.

"Well, Mrs. Kat found a jar of eyeballs, which is why I took over going through the box. She wanted to buy the eyeballs, because they were epic."

"I'm sure they were," Detective Keeler said in an admirably even tone of voice.

"I found a garland of guts—which was fake, of course," Henry continued. "I wanted to keep that, but I knew Dad would say no."

"Thank the Lord above," I muttered under my breath.

"There were some fake potion bottles. They were plastic and the labels were pretty worn. A set of lights in the shape of jack-o-lanterns. A whole bag of plastic vampire teeth. A zombie makeup kit that hadn't even been opened. And the bones."

"How many bones?" Keeler asked. "Can you describe them?"

Henry shrugged. "Then there was a foot with some wires holding the little bones together. And maybe ten or fifteen other bones of different sizes. And the skull. It kinda freaked me out because it was sooo realistic."

Keeler glanced over at me.

"The ones that were obviously Styrofoam or plastic I left in the sale," I replied. "Anything else I took in to Doctor Basava. Some I felt certain were resin reproductions, but I wanted to make sure."

The detective nodded, then turned back to Henry. "Can you tell me anything about the box itself? What things were packed in?"

"Everything was wrapped in white tissue paper or newspaper. Local newspaper, because I glanced at a story about the high school football team." He frowned. "I didn't recognize any of the names so I'm thinking the paper was from more than a couple of years ago. The skull wasn't wrapped in paper or anything. Neither were any of the other bones."

Keeler glanced over at me and I winced. "We got rid of all the paper. Recycling picked it up this morning."

The detective sighed, and made a note on his pad of paper. "Do you remember anything about the box, Henry?"

Henry thought for a second then slowly shook his head. "It was a box. I think it had some writing on it, and a picture, but I can't remember what it was."

My phone beeped and I looked at the text from Kat. "My friend thinks it was a grocery store produce box or something, but she's not sure. She said the same as Henry about the newspaper wrapping and the contents."

"Thanks." Keeler made a few notes. "Can you send me her contact information, just in case I need to speak with her?"

I nodded and wrote the information down on a sticky note, passing it to the detective. He put it in his notebook. "Who brought the boxes in and stacked them?" he asked me.

"Whoever was home at the time they were dropped off," I replied. "The volunteer bringing the boxes would help bring them in as well."

"Were the boxes stacked near each other? Were they moved after they were dropped off?" he continued.

"They were stacked wherever we had room, which wasn't always next to each other. And they were shifted and moved around throughout the week." I blew out a breath, frustrated that we didn't have more to help the detective. It wasn't like I'd realized something in the boxes would be part of a murder investigation when I was trying to clear a path to the various parts of my home.

Then I remembered something. The ghost had appeared Thursday night. There was a chance that the box with the skull had arrived before then, and the spirit just hadn't made her presence known until Thursday night, but I suspected otherwise.

"I...I don't have a concrete reason to believe this, but I think the box was delivered sometime Thursday. That would mean the box either came from Bert's donors, J.T.'s donors, Molly's donors, or Daisy's donors. J.T. is positive his two donation boxes only held books and ties, so I'd probably focus on the other three's lists first."

Keeler glanced up at me. "Molly? Bert? Daisy?"

I wrote down everyone's full names and contact info and passed it to him. "You have Molly's list already. I should have Daisy's by tomorrow and Bert's soon."

He nodded, then looked around. "Anything else?"

No one had anything to add, so Detective Keeler thanked us for our time, shook Judge Beck's hand, then left.

"All right, kids." Heather clapped her hands. "We need to get back and get going on the homework." She turned to the judge and me. "Thank you both for the pizza and hospitality. I hope they catch whoever killed that poor woman."

Me too, I thought as we walked them to the door.

CHAPTER 14

*A*fter they left, the judge and I finished cleaning up the kitchen and putting away the remaining left-overs. He volunteered to take Cagney for her walk. I took the opportunity to unpack my laptop and some files, and spread them across the dining room table. I'd taken the morning off to go see Doctor Basava, and was now behind on the work that actually paid the bills. J.T. was intrigued by the whole mystery-of-the-skull, and was already planning his next episode of "Gator, Private Eye" with himself in the lead investigative role. He was clearly supportive of my little side-sleuthing—but I knew that would only be if I could keep on top of the business's work by putting in extra hours in the evenings as well as on weekends. I was no stranger to unpaid overtime, and this wasn't truly overtime given that I'd come in at close to noon.

Plus the judge and I had kind of built our relationship on late-night side-by-side work at the dining room table. He was only a partially reformed workaholic, and I didn't even claim to be partially reformed. The kids weren't here this week, and sitting beside the judge as we both worked was strangely romantic. Well, romantic for me.

Carly Billings. Molly was convinced that the skull belonged to our town's only cold case, and I felt the same. Putting my work-work aside for a moment, I ran a quick search on the girl, looking at her credit report and social media at the time of her disappearance, as well as a case search. Her credit report was bare, the only entries from her cell phone carrier, her auto insurance, and her sources of income. Three part-time jobs. I winced at that, remembering how difficult it was to make decent money right after high school. The girl had clearly been a hard-worker to put in those hours, racing from one job to another.

Noting the car insurance entry, I ran motor vehicle data on her 2002 Ford Escort. Surprisingly she must have bought it for cash since there was no sign of a loan on her credit report. Although I knew that lots of used car lots did their own financing on older vehicles and didn't always report the information to the credit bureaus. Carly didn't have any speeding tickets on her record. There were a few parking violations, and almost a dozen equipment repair orders. Headlight out. License plate light out. Muffler missing. Tail light out.

Having an old persnickety car myself, I felt for the girl.

Her case search was squeaky clean, which I had hoped it would be for a twenty-year-old girl. Her social media was spotty. She had an old Facebook profile that no one had shut down, but hadn't posted much on it before her disappearance. She'd been tagged in a few of her friends' pictures, so I noted down the friends' names and pulled up the images.

Carly had been a pretty girl with a round face, straight light brown hair, and girl-next-door looks. Her smile was radiant, bringing a dimple to her left cheek and a sparkle to her green eyes. My heart hurt looking at these photos, thinking of a lively, vibrant girl who probably never lived to see her twenty-first birthday.

I stared at her picture, then closed the browser tab. This was too painful to look at, to even think about. The images made me think of Violet, of Molly, of Madison in a few years. I wanted long lives for all those women—for everyone. And I wanted the same for Carly Billings, but after five years of being missing, I doubted she'd lived past the age of twenty.

My heart hurt for her, but I closed all of the tabs and turned to the work-work instead. There was no proof that the skull I'd found was Carly's, and while I yearned to investigate her disappearance, I had other things to do. Tomorrow I'd look at the lists of donations, dig a bit deeper, and if the Carly Billings's case and the investigation about the skull converged, then I'd go down that rabbit hole. Until then, there was a potential fraud case I needed to work on.

I was deep into researching the fraud investigation when I heard the front door open. Cagney came into the dining room, her tags jingling on her collar, her mouth open and tongue practically dragging. She propped her front paws on my thigh and greeted me with a smile and a tail wag so enthusiastic that her whole rear end swayed from side-to-side. Taco, who was sitting next to my laptop on a pile of folders eyed the puppy with disdain.

"Did you have a nice walk?" I asked, ruffling Cagney's floppy ears. Her tail double-timed at the word "walk" even though she looked exhausted.

Judge Beck walked into the dining room, pulling his worn T-shirt off and wiping his face with it. He looked equally exhausted.

"Did you go for a walk, or jog to Milford and back?" I teased.

"Cagney was practically dragging me down the street, so I decided a run would be better than a walk. We didn't make it to Milford and back, but my watch says we did three miles before I convinced her to drop the pace a bit."

My eyes widened. "Three *miles*? Three blocks would be the extent of any running I could do, and even then I'd probably need to call for an ambulance at the end of it all."

He grinned sheepishly and patted his flat stomach. "Golf season is coming up. I need to get in shape."

"For *golf*?" I stared at him, wondering what sort of golfing he intended to do where running three miles with a dog was a reasonable training regime. As far as I knew, Judge Beck and his buddies always got golf carts, so it wasn't like he was going to be lugging his clubs around eighteen holes.

"Yes, golf."

He walked closer and it suddenly registered that he didn't have a shirt on. And that a shirtless Judge Beck looked *really* good. He wasn't sculpted or muscle-bound, but he was clearly fit, and I couldn't help my eyes from roaming across his broad chest, down his flat stomach, and along the waistband of the navy sweatpants hugging his hips.

Suddenly all thoughts of fraud vanished from my head. The judge and I had done a lot of kissing in the last two months. Kissing. Cuddling. A little roaming of the hands. But that had been it and I knew that the both of us were way past ready to take our relationship into the bedroom. We were mature adults. His divorce was final. I knew that Eli would have wanted me to find love again, and that he would have approved heartily of Judge Beck. The kids thought we were "cute." I wasn't sure what was holding us back. We definitely restrained ourselves when the kids were here. A "cute" kiss or hug was one thing, but neither of us wanted Madison or Henry to accidently catch us in the middle of something X-rated—or catch us coming out of each other's bedrooms in the early morning. The every-other-week thing meant we always felt like we were awkwardly starting anew each second Monday. But while the physical part of our relationship was two steps forward, one step back, the emotional part had only grown stronger. And the delay in our making love had built the sexual tension between us to an excruciating level of attraction.

"What are you working on?" he murmured, leaning over me to look at my laptop.

I rested my head against his stomach, having to think for a second about what I'd been doing before he and Cagney had come into the room.

"There's a local church that suspects fraud in one or more of their charitable outreach programs. I'm digging through their contracts and accounting reports and wishing I had Violet here to help me. When it comes to accounting, I'm kind of in the dark."

"You're sharp and good at spotting patterns and discrepancies." He leaned down to kiss the top of my head. "I'm sure you'll be able to figure it out without Violet."

"If not, I'll ask J.T. if we can throw some contractor dollars at her." I sighed, losing all interest in work as the judge's arms came around me.

He kissed me on the top of the head once more, squeezed my shoulders, then went to pull away. "I'll leave you to your work."

"No!" I grabbed his arms. "I'll do it tomorrow. I'd rather spend some time with you tonight."

He hesitated. "I've got some work I probably should do as well."

Making a decision, I closed the lid on my laptop and stood, stepping toward him and putting my hands on his waist. "Can it wait? Because I'd really like us...I mean, I'd love if we..."

He frowned. "I'm sweaty. And I smell. I should probably take a shower."

"You're fine." He was. His sweat had that light masculine smell combined with soap and deodorant that was oddly appealing. I'd never been into the jocks, but a sweaty Judge Beck was irresistible.

He sucked in a breath as my hands slowly moved up his sides. "Are you sure? I mean, *I'm* sure, but I want to take it slow. You're important to me, Kay. I care about you. I want you. But I know you lost Eli only a little over a year ago. Your love for him was deep—it still is. Plus we're friends. I live here. My children adore you. I don't want to cross a line and jeopardize what we have."

I stood on my tip-toes, leaned forward, and kissed his collarbone. "We're adults. I love Madison and Henry and whatever happens between us won't affect my feelings for them. And if you're bad in bed, then we'll just try again another time," I teased. "I'm all about second chances. And third and fourth chances, if that's necessary."

He laughed, pulling me tight against him. "I am *not* bad in bed."

"Prove it." My head spun a little as his hands caressed my back then skated down my body. "The kids aren't here. Cagney is worn out after her run, so she probably won't be bothering us. I'm ready. Unless that three miles wore you out as well?"

He made a noise low in his throat, half laugh and half growl. "It takes more than a three mile run to wear me out. I'm getting a second wind here."

I smiled pressing myself against him and lifting my face to his. "So…your room or mine?"

CHAPTER 15

I woke before dawn, a little spoon curled up against Judge Beck. His breath stirred my hair, his hands holding me tight.

Last night had been amazing.

He'd been amazing.

I hoped that I'd been amazing as well.

As much as I would have loved to sleep in, and maybe to wake up for a round two, I hadn't cancelled with Daisy and she would be coming through the door in the next ten or fifteen minutes for our sunrise yoga.

I opened my eyes and looked into Cagney's brown orbs. She was sitting at the edge of the king-sized bed, staring at me intently.

The dog was clearly confused about what was going on here. I had to admit I was a little confused as well, but that happy glow made me willing to just go with it, in spite of the uncertainty that lay before us. I got the feeling we were hovering at the edge of that "L" word. Honestly, I was already in love, but I knew that it would take time to see how deep our feelings went before I said the word.

Cagney didn't seem as concerned about our emotional connections or what sort of activities the judge and I had been into last night. She was probably only curious about why I was in this bed and not in my own room.

A yowl sounded outside in the hallway and I realized Cagney wasn't the only one disturbed by the change in routine. Taco slept in my bed with me every night, and while he apparently hadn't been all that bothered about having the mattress to himself, he was now ready for breakfast and annoyed that I wasn't where I was supposed to be—which was in the kitchen, putting food into his bowl.

I slid out from under the judge's arm and leg, trying not to wake him. He grumbled in his sleep and turned over while I searched in the dark for my discarded clothing, finally giving up and sneaking back to my room to throw on my yoga attire. By this point Taco was weaving around my legs, purring and making it really difficult for me to get dressed.

I finally managed to get my pants and sports bra on before grabbing a T-shirt and my sneakers and heading downstairs. Priority one was obviously to feed the cat. Priority two was to get the coffee started. It had just begun to brew when I heard Cagney's nails on the stairs. Pulling her bag of food from under the sink, I put some in her bowl, careful to separate the dog and the cat. Neither one liked to share—especially Taco. We'd had a few issues early on when Cagney had gulped down her food in record time and nearly got a face full of cat claws trying to steal Taco's food. And the cat was just as bad, hissing at Cagney and helping himself to the dog chow while Cagney stood aside and watched with sad and hungry eyes.

Separating them and monitoring the dining situation had worked. I still liked to keep an eye on the two of them, but they both seemed to be getting into the habit of respecting each other's food bowls.

Cagney was just giving her bowl one last lick when her head shot up. A second later I heard the back gate and the pup raced to the back door, jumping up and down in her eagerness to get out. I peeked through the back window to make sure Daisy and Lady were inside the yard and the gate was shut, then let my dog out.

Taco was still picking through his food, trying to only eat the Happy Cat and avoid the diet kibble, so I decided to leave him inside this morning. Grabbing my mat and my water bottle, I headed outside.

Daisy and I spread out our mats as the dogs chased each other around the backyard. We'd just begun our first Sun Salutation when Daisy halted, regarding me with narrowed eyes.

"What?" I asked, feeling the blush snake up my neck and across my face.

"You're having sex," Daisy announced with a laugh.

"Shhh!" I cast a quick glance back at the house.

"Shhh?" She laughed again. "Why the need for silence? I assume Judge Beck was your partner in this activity, so he already knows you were doing the deed. Is there some other beau I don't know about? Is that why you don't want the judge to know you're getting some action?"

"Yes. I mean, of course it's Judge Beck. I just don't want him hearing us gossiping about it." I was so flustered. And, to my credit, still holding my plank pose.

"Kay is getting busy. Kay is getting busy," Daisy chanted, thankfully swooping into a cobra position. "Was it good? You look twenty years younger, so I'm assuming it was incredible."

"I do not look twenty years younger," I countered. "And let's just say that I'm very happy this morning. And I hope to be equally happy tomorrow morning as well."

"I'm hoping you're late to work and doubly happy." Daisy grinned at me from her downward dog.

"Stop." Now I was the one laughing. "I can't do yoga and talk about this."

"Then let's skip yoga so you can give me all the details."

I rolled my eyes. "No details. I'm not a kiss-and-tell sort of woman."

"That's so unfair! I told you all about J.T. and me when we finally got around to doing the mattress mambo," she pointed out.

"Yes you did, even though I didn't want to hear it. He's my *boss*, Daisy. I don't need to know what underwear he prefers or that he likes to talk dirty. I can't scrub those images from my mind, no matter how hard I try."

"Please give me some images to attempt to scrub from my mind. Please." Daisy glanced over at me. "At least tell me if he's a boxers or briefs guy. Or those boxer-briefs? Sweet goddess, does he go commando?"

My face was on fire. "I'm not saying."

Daisy squealed. "He *does* go commando! Big spoon or little spoon? Is he a cuddler, or does he need his space in the bed?"

"Can we just focus on yoga? And move out of downward dog before I collapse?"

"You are no fun," Daisy complained.

"That's not what he said." I grinned.

"Oh, that's so unfair! Tease."

I sighed. "It was amazing. And in spite of it being so long since I've made love, I seemed to have remembered how to do it. Guess it's like riding a bike."

Daisy chuckled. "Better than riding a bike. But I get what you mean. Saturday night, J.T. and I—"

"No!" I interrupted. "I don't want to hear all the interesting kinks you and *my boss* are doing, Daisy. I'm glad you both are in love and making love, but I don't need to know the details."

"Fine, fine." Daisy laughed. "I'm happy for you, Kay. I like the judge, and think you both are a wonderful couple. And I'm happy you're getting some."

We finished our yoga and herded the dogs inside, putting up a baby gate to keep them in the foyer as we had coffee. Hearing the judge's footsteps on the stairs, I poured a third cup and handed it to him as he came into the kitchen.

Our fingers brushed as he took the cup and I felt that zing, just like in the romance novels.

He read his coffee mug. "*Silently judging you.*"

It was one of the novelty mugs I'd gotten from the yard sale. Mine said *Cat Mom* under a stylized graphic of an orange tabby. Daisy had selected one that said *This might be wine.*

"Have you ever *silently* judged someone?" Daisy asked the judge.

He smiled. "In the court room? No. But outside the court-room I've found it's sometimes best to keep my opinions to myself."

"I couldn't decide whether to put your coffee in that one, or the one that says *Not my circus, not my monkeys,*" I told him.

"He should take that one to work," Daisy pointed out. "And display it while he's on the bench."

"Except when I'm on the bench, it *is* my circus, and they *are* my monkeys," the judge pointed out.

He turned to pour some creamer in his coffee, and Daisy pointedly looked at his rear, then nodded at me approvingly.

Stop, I mouthed, elbowing her.

"Are these the coffee cups you got from the yard sale?" the judge asked as he turned around.

"Yes. The yard sale." I shot Daisy a warning glance and she

snickered before taking a sip of her coffee. "Uh, what do you want to do for dinner tonight?"

I'd never felt so flustered in my life. I eyed Daisy, trying to subtly get her out of here before she got caught eyeing the judge's butt, or worse, asked him what sort of underwear he wore. Daisy must have gotten the message, because she took a larger gulp of her coffee.

"I should be home a bit early tonight. I can put those pork chops in the oven before I take Cagney out for a walk," the judge replied.

"That sounds good." I made a face at Daisy and she rolled her eyes. "We can have a salad with them. Maybe I'll roast some carrots."

Daisy gulped her coffee and set the mug on the counter. "As much as I'd like to stay for this stimulating dinner-plan conversation, I need to get going."

I blew out a breath, thankful that my friend had taken pity on me and was cutting our morning social time short.

"Plus, I'm sure you two lovebirds have lots of naughty things you'd rather discuss than pork chops, and I'm definitely a third wheel."

My eyes widened.

"Don't do anything I wouldn't do," Daisy instructed as she turned to leave the kitchen. "But since I'm up for all the kinky stuff, that doesn't really limit you two. Just remember your safe-words."

Daisy and Lady headed toward the door. I turned to see the judge eyeing me with something that could only be called a smirk on his face.

"You told her?" he asked.

He didn't seem upset about Daisy knowing we'd taken our relationship into the bedroom. I was grateful for that. He could be a very private man, and I wasn't sure how much he wanted out in the open. But Daisy *was* my best friend, and the judge had been rather demonstrative with me at our Friday happy hours, so I was going to assume this was all okay.

"Daisy guessed," I told him. "Evidently I look twenty years younger this morning."

"You *do* look amazing." He stepped forward and wrapped his arms around me.

I laughed. "Slick side-step there, buddy. I'm well aware that I do not look twenty years younger, but I'm very happy. I'm hoping we make this a regular thing."

"I plan on it." He bent down and kissed me. "If I didn't have an eight o'clock trial, I'd suggest we play hooky."

"If I didn't have a fraud case and a stack of process-serving research, I'd absolutely play hooky," I told him.

"Them I'll just have to anticipate tonight."

He kissed me once more, and when he pulled away, I found I *really* wished we could stay home today.

"Tonight," I promised him.

He picked up his coffee, hesitating as he turned to leave. "Kay? Should we have safe-words?"

"Uh...maybe?" I squeaked, feeling more like I was sixteen than sixty-one. "Eventually. Although I'd kind of like to stick to the basic stuff for now."

He grinned, saluting me with his coffee. "Basic stuff it is."

I watched him go, my gaze also drifting to his rear. Then I laughed, shook my head, and forced myself to get ready for work.

CHAPTER 16

$\mathcal{I}$ was just pulling out of the driveway when my phone rang. When I saw it was Henry, I put the car in park and answered it.

"Are you okay?" I asked, worried that there was some reason he hadn't called his father or his mother.

"Yeah I'm fine." The sound of kids in the background told me he was at school. "I was thinking about the skull and the box last night and I remember what the writing was on the box. Something like McClain's Apples, or McCrory's Orchard or something. It had a picture of an apple on the box under the words."

An apple. I remembered the ghost in the corner of my kitchen, and how she kept rolling the apple from the fruit basket. It had to be important—both the apple, and the logo on the box. The ghost had been trying to tell me something. A clue. And that clue had to do with the orchard.

I yanked a notepad out of my bag and jotted the names down, putting a question mark behind each of them.

"How positive are you that it was an apple on the box?

That the name was on the box that had the skull?" I asked him.

Kat had also said she'd thought it was a produce box, and Henry knew this was important and a serious matter. But still, I felt I should ask.

"Um, I'm seventy percent sure? It might have been the box with the other Halloween stuff in it, but I'm pretty positive the orchard name and the apple were on the one with the skull."

Seventy percent was worth calling Detective Keeler and letting him know.

"Thanks Henry," I said. "Let your father or me know if you think of anything else. And have a good day at school."

"Thanks Miss Kay. Talk to you later."

He hung up and I dialed the number for Detective Keeler. When someone else answered the phone, I blinked in surprise. Then I recognized the voice—Detective Toots.

"Is Detective Keeler in?" I asked reluctant to talk to Toots about anything, let alone a murder investigation.

"He's out. Can I take a message?" Toots asked, sounding like taking a message was the last thing he wanted to do.

"Please tell him that Kay Carrera called. The judge's son thinks the name on the box where the skull was found might be from an apple orchard—McClain's, or McCrory's. He also thinks there was a picture of an apple on the box."

There was a long silence. Just as I was about to ask if he was still on the line, Toots spoke up.

"Okay. I'll have him call you when he gets in."

The call disconnected before I could give him my number, leaving me with little faith that Keeler would get the message at all. Pulling out of the driveway, I headed in to work, mulling over the case and deciding that I should probably try to reach Keeler again if he hadn't gotten back to me by the end of the day.

Would it matter, though? In the big-picture scheme of things, maybe, but as a potential clue, the name on the box didn't seem like it was all that important. I felt it was important because a ghost had been rolling an apple across my kitchen counter for the few days the skull was in my possession, but without that bit of information, it was just a box—a box anyone could have picked up anywhere. Detective Keeler probably wouldn't bother following up on that—not when he had all those lists of donors to go through.

Perhaps the killer just happened to buy some produce there once years ago. Or maybe he got the box from a friend or out of a neighborhood recycle bin when he was looking for cheap storage options. Going to the orchard and asking questions of the owners didn't seem like it would yield much. Plus Keeler had enough to do trying to track down who the donor was.

Going through the lists I'd had our volunteers compile about who donated items for the yard sale did seem like a much better use of investigative time, but I hated to leave any stone unturned. As I pulled into the parking lot at work, I was considering whether I should try to locate the orchard's actual name and maybe visit them myself.

Maybe the killer worked for the orchard, or was a regular customer. Apples were important. The orchard was important. At least the ghost thought so, and in the last year, I'd learned to pay attention when a ghost tried to tell me something.

J.T. pulled in beside me. We both got out of our cars, but he reached back in and pulled a box of donuts out of the back seat. "I figured with everything going on, you might not have a whole lot of time to bake."

"You figured right." Between the visit from Detective Keeler, work, and some quality time with the judge, baking had been the last thing on my mind.

"Besides," he continued as we walked to the office. "I figure I owe you since I want to hear all about The Case of the Missing Skull."

I bit back a smile. "That's the name of your episode? I mean, the skull wasn't missing, so maybe you should title it The Case of the Found Skull, or maybe The Case of the Mysterious Skull."

"How about The Case of the Yard Sale Skull?" J.T. balanced the donut box in one hand and held the door for me with the other.

"Now that has a catchy ring to it."

"You're here!" Molly exclaimed as we came in. Then her gaze shifted to the box in J.T.'s hands. "Ooo, donuts!"

"The jelly-filled is mine," J.T. said as he put the box next to the coffee maker. "Everything else is up for grabs."

We all picked out a donut and got our coffee while I went over what had happened last night and my call with Henry this morning.

"McCray's Orchard," Molly volunteered. "It's off of Route Sixteen. Cute place. They do most of their business during the summer, but they keep their store open off-season to sell cider, jellies, pies, and stuff. I'm kinda surprised they're still in business since they're off the beaten track a bit. I'm pretty sure the McCrays have owned it for a couple of generations."

I thought of Suzette and how the developers had wanted her property. It probably was the same with the orchard. But just as family and tradition had weighed into Suzette's decision not to sell the remaining part of her family's farm, I was sure the same were keeping the McCrays struggling along with their business.

"I don't see where the box has anything to do with this," J.T. grumbled. "It could be just an old box someone brought apples home in and then used to store stuff. The killer and

119

the victim might have had nothing to do with McCray's Orchard."

I would have thought the same if I hadn't had a ghost rolling apples across my kitchen counter.

"It's still a clue," Molly said. "It might not make sense now, but there could be other clues that come to light that all fit together like a jigsaw puzzle. Maybe the killer worked there, or was a repeat customer. Maybe the logo on the box will help date when the skull was put in there, or something."

J.T. shot her a skeptical look. "That's a real stretch, Molly."

Before she could defend her theory, Miles walked in. After greeting us, he made a beeline for the donuts.

"Donut tax involves you telling us what you know about The Case of the Yard Sale Skull," J.T. informed the deputy.

"There's not much to tell. We don't have a positive ID on the skull yet and probably won't have one for at least a few days, if not a few weeks," Miles said as he snagged a donut with pink icing and sprinkles from the box. "We've narrowed down a list of women in the approximate age range who went missing between three and ten years ago from within the state. It's a pretty daunting list—even more daunting if we expand it nation-wide."

"Has Keeler tagged you to help?" I asked him. "Or Toots?"

Everyone shuddered at the name.

"Keeler knows better than to ask Toots to do anything," Miles replied in between bites of donut. "I'm going through the list of the missing women—when they were last seen and where. I even put up a map with push-pins and strings, trying to see if any of them could have been in the area."

"It's Carly Billings," Molly insisted. "Come on, guys. She was twenty. She went missing five years ago right here in Locust Point. It's her."

Miles looked down at the last bit of his donut, focusing his gaze anywhere but on us. "Maybe. She's on the list. But just because the skull was found in the area and the timeline overlaps, doesn't mean it's her. I'd be a pretty bad future detective if I didn't look at other possible women as the victim."

I felt bad for Miles, caught between the need to keep certain things confidential and the donut tax.

"So, putting the whole 'who does the skull belong to' aside, how *did* the victim's skull end up in a box of Halloween decorations?" I asked. "The murderer wouldn't have hidden her body in random boxes in the attic where decomposition would have alerted the residents and probably the neighbors. So that means it must have been moved there from its original burial place."

J.T. frowned. "That's a good question. And why move it? Why hide the body in a place where it hasn't been discovered for however long it took to decompose, only to risk everything by digging it up and relocating it? Especially to what I assume is the killer's own house?"

"Maybe animals scattered the remains, some kid found it, thought it was a cool fake and brought it home to stuff it in a box in the attic," Miles pointed out. "We can't know for certain that the person who had possession of the skull was the murderer, or even knew that the skull was real."

"Henry knew something was wrong the moment he picked it up," I told Miles. "So did Kat. I can't believe a family has been using a real skull as a Halloween decoration and no one knew."

"So the person who had it in the box knew, and accidentally gave it away?" J.T. shook his head. "I can't imagine something like that. It's not like forgetting where you put your keys. You'd *know* that the box of Halloween decorations is where you put the skull of the woman you murdered five years ago."

I remembered my conversation with Bert about the golf

clubs. "So his wife accidently gave the box away when he was at work, because *she* didn't know what was in it."

Everyone murmured agreement that the theory was sound.

"But back to my original question: why move the body? Did someone find the murderer's original hiding place? Or was he waiting for it the body to decompose so he could take the skull home as some sort of sick trophy? Hiding it in a box of holiday stuff so his wife didn't know?"

"That's disgusting," Molly informed me. "Although that whole trophy thing does happen according to the true crime shows I've watched on TV."

"That's not the only question," I continued. "Where's the rest of her body? The skull was the only real bone in the box. Are the rest of the bones in other boxes in the attic? Are they still in the original burial place?"

Molly held up her hands. "I'm just sayin' that if I was the murderer, I'd be getting rid of those other bones real fast. Soon as I found out the skull was gone, I'd realize I had limited time before the police might be knocking on my door with a search warrant."

I felt a chill at the thought. My garage had been broken into Friday night. Was the murderer trying to retrieve the skull? Had he shown up at the yard sale looking for it? If so, then Molly was right and he'd probably disposed of the other bones yesterday. Even if we found out where the box came from, the police might not find anything at the house to tie the residents to the murder. And as we'd just been discussing, there were plenty of plausible reasons that someone might have innocently come into possession of a skull for there to be reasonable doubt in a trial.

J.T. scowled. "As much as I wanted it to be otherwise, I can't see how the boyfriend could possibly have been the murderer unless he had an accomplice who stayed in the area and moved the skull from its original burial place."

"Yeah, I was hoping it was the boyfriend as well, but since he's in Florida, he's not here moving bodies and hiding skulls in attics," Molly grumbled.

"The killer might not even still be alive," Miles pointed out. "Maybe he died and his wife had no idea it was in the box, or that it was real. Or maybe the house was sold and the box of stuff got left behind in the attic for the new owners. If people have medical skeletons in their attics from three generations ago, then whoever owns the house now might be in the dark about the crime."

That idea bothered me. I hated the thought that a murderer might never be made to pay for his crime, that the victim and her family might never receive justice. Perhaps knowing what happened and being able to bury what remained of their daughter might give the family some closure, but for me that would never be enough.

"I'm assuming Keeler is off interviewing the donors from the lists?" I asked Miles, thinking that might be why the detective hadn't been in when I'd called.

"Please tell me he's at least interviewing Carly Billings's parents," Molly interjected. "I know you're skeptical, but I really think it's her."

"He is going through the lists. We haven't narrowed down the victim yet," Miles repeated. "Keeler is probably going to wait until the DNA comes in, but in the meantime I'm doing the prep work."

His chest puffed out a bit at that and I smiled. "I'm sure you're doing a very thorough job. You'll make a great detective, Miles."

"That's pretty far in the future," he said, squirming at the praise. "And it depends on whether Keeler stays and how fast we can get Toots to leave."

"Given Toots should be standing in the unemployment line, he can't leave fast enough for me," Molly drawled.

Conversation turned to a litany of Toots's general ineptness, and I opened the file on the fraud case I was investigating. My mind kept straying to the skull, and Carly Billings even after Miles and J.T. left.

McCray's Orchard. I'd thought about going there on my lunch hour and asking around, but now I had a different idea.

"Do you think your friend's sister would talk to me about Carly?" I asked Molly.

She swiveled around to face me, surprised at the question. "Sure. She was really upset about the whole thing. Let me get her number and text her and see if she's available. Last I heard she'd just had twins, so she might like an adult visitor."

By lunch Molly had a name, address, and phone number for me.

"Halley Powers said if you show up in the next half an hour with chicken enchiladas from Taco Bonanza, she'll not only talk with you, she'll consider giving you one of the twins." Molly laughed at my grimace. "I told her you'd pass on the kid. Then I went ahead and ordered 2 chicken enchilada lunch specials to go. Leave now and you'll have time to swing by before heading to Halley's."

I thanked Molly, grabbed my purse and ran out the door. In twenty minutes I was pulling into the driveway that my co-worker had jotted down on a sticky note, the delicious aroma of chicken enchiladas filling my car.

CHAPTER 17

*H*alley Powers answered the door with one baby on her hip and the other making their displeasure loudly known from behind her in the living room. She was tall, a good bit of skin showing between the hem of her capris yoga pants and her hot pink socks. Half of her dark hair had escaped its messy bun, wavy locks dangling along the nape of her neck and in her eyes. Her hot pink shirt had been washed more times than the manufacturer had probably intended and was shapeless, with a stretched-out neckline and some stains along both shoulders that I recognized from when my friends had been home with their babies.

The babe-in-arms looked to be around six months old and was wearing a striped onesie. He—or she—kicked their chubby legs and eyed me intently, while their sibling howled for attention.

"Bless you." She reached out a hand to take one of the bags of take-out. "I mean it. Seriously. Bless you. If I had to eat stale crackers, cheddar cheese, and bologna one more day I was going to put my head in the oven. Kirk's been working doubles for the last five days and I haven't been able to get someone to watch the twins while I grocery shop." She ushered me in and I followed her as she spoke. "Taking them to the store with me is not an option. Trust me. I tried it once and it was a disaster. Had to abandon my cart and get out of there before the employees and customers chased me out with torches and pitchforks. I'm pretty tight with a buck, but I'm at the point where I'm considering one of those online grocery delivery services."

She put the one baby in a playpen and I saw the definition of her arm muscles under that shirt. Impressive. Evidently caring for twins was the equivalent of arm day at the gym.

"I'm sure your husband wouldn't mind," I said, even though I had no idea if that was true or not. If the guy had been working doubles, then I assumed he was getting at least time-and-a-half pay.

"Oh he wouldn't. In fact, he'd insist on it. Like I said, I'm the cheap one in this marriage. We're getting out of here and buying a house in the next year if I have to pimp myself on the corner. Or sell a kidney." Halley reached down and grabbed a binkie off the coffee table, offering it to the upset twin. The baby eagerly took it and suddenly became content.

I smiled, liking this young woman. "I really appreciate you meeting with me on such short notice. Bringing lunch wasn't a problem—I'm hungry as well.

"Then let's eat, girl! Come on into the dining room here. These hoodlums should give us a generous ten minutes to bolt this food down before they demand my attention once more."

I followed her, impressed at the relative neatness of the house. Yes, there were baby toys, bouncers, swings, and play mats everywhere. Burp rags were decoratively draped over chairs and the sofa. But the place was clean, and smelled lemony fresh.

We sat at a table after Halley moved several stacks of

papers and a planner to the side. The woman didn't waste any time digging into her food, so I didn't stand on ceremony either. I guess with twins, you ate as fast as you could whenever you got the chance. And as she said, the twins would probably start crying any minute now.

"You wanted to talk about Carly?" She held a hand over her mouth, talking as she chewed. "Go ahead. After all these years I'm just happy she wasn't forgotten. *I've* never forgotten her. I never will. She's in my prayers every night, and I'm not exactly a religious woman, you know."

"How did you know Carly?" I pulled a notepad from my purse, took a quick bite and grabbed my pen.

"We worked together at the Style Stable. Remember that place? Super cheap clothing. If you were on a budget, it was the place to go to grab some clothes for that new office job, or a weekend on the shore, or as a step up from jeans and T-shirts. Not that I wear anything fancier than yoga pants these days. I'm lucky if I manage to get a shower and change out of my pajamas."

"Did she go to Milford High?" I asked.

Halley shook her head. "Her family moved her when she was eighteen. I think they were originally from some place in the Midwest. She never talked a lot about where she grew up. I know her family fell on hard times and lost their house to foreclosure. Her dad got a job offer in Milford at the cannery, so the family came here. She confessed to me that they were living in the back of their SUV and in tents for the first few months until her dad got enough of his pay to put a security deposit and one month's rent on a one-bedroom apartment. Carly slept on a pull-out in the living room, but it was better than a tent. That girl worked three jobs trying to save enough money for classes at the community college and maybe eventually a place of her own. It was crazy. She slept in four-hour segments because of her shifts. I was worried she'd burn out, but she was full of energy, enthusiasm, and optimism. She wanted to enroll in the nursing program. I think she would have been a great nurse. Carly could hustle, and she was kind and even-tempered. Her smile was like sunshine on a gloomy day."

"Tell me about her boyfriend," I asked, alternating between taking notes and eating my enchiladas.

"Memphis Brookstone." Halley's eyes just about rolled right out of her head as she said the name. "Sounds like a prep-school dude, doesn't he? But he was far from prep-school, let me tell you. Totally hot. Totally worthless. Carly was a pretty girl. If she was smart, she would have gotten a sugar daddy and been off the couch and in college with a wink of her eye. But I guess hormones don't always align with self-interest. I'm lucky. I fell for Kirk hard and that was it for me. He didn't have more than a couple of bucks to rub together, but he's ambitious and hard-working, and smart. We may not end up billionaires or even hundred-thousand-aires, but we'll be stable and comfortable, and have college funds for the twins as well as 401k accounts for us. Memphis? All that guy was going to do was sit on someone's couch and complain about how the world had done him wrong. You could bounce a quarter off that guy's abs, and he had some serious bedroom eyes, but he was not a guy to pin your future on."

A grumbly noise and a grunt came from the living room.

"I kept telling Carly to ditch him, and I think in the end she was actually thinking about it. Memphis wanted to go to Florida and do who-knows-what. She wasn't a dumb girl. She knew there was no future with him, and as sexy as that man was, Carly wanted a future."

"I heard she broke up with him a few days before she vanished?" I asked, wondering if there was some way in spite of the logistics to make the boyfriend a suspect once more.

"She never told me that." Halley shrugged. "One day she was going to ditch him and find someone more stable, someone with a future. The next day she was all about his dark eyes and biceps. Honestly? I think she would have left him the moment a more suitable guy winked at her. But working three jobs at minimum wage isn't exactly the environment to find a stable boyfriend. It's not like a bunch of eligible guys shop at the Style Stable."

I wondered for a brief second how Halley had met *her* husband, but some noises from the living room reminded me I had a limited window of time to ask questions about Carly.

"Tell me about the night Carly went missing." I crammed another bite of enchilada into my mouth and eyed the twins with trepidation.

Halley pushed the empty container away from her and sighed, patting her stomach. "It was five years ago that Carly vanished. Five years. We were both twenty. She'd been my best friend for two years. I don't know what happened to her and it haunts me. If she was going to run away with Memphis, she would have told me. Even if it was a spur-of-the-moment thing, she would have told me. And even then, I don't think she would have done that. He was sex-on-a-stick hot, but like I said, Carly had a practical streak. His washboard abs might have put her brain in a twist, but not enough for her to give up everything she'd been working for, to head south in a dilapidated truck with no job and no money besides what she had in savings. She'd already been through that with her parents, and I'm positive she never would have chosen that kind of life, no matter how hot Memphis was."

"So he asked her to go with him. She said no, and he decided to take her anyway." I watched Halley to see how that landed.

She snorted. "Nope. Memphis was a wimp. He probably did ask her to go because Carly had some money saved and he wanted that money as much as he wanted her warming his bed. But if she said no, he would have just found someone else to ride shotgun in that rusted truck. It wasn't him. I hate the guy, but he's not a killer. He doesn't have it in him."

"Then who?" I asked, hearing more noise from the living room.

She held up her hands. "If I knew that, there would be someone in jail right now. Or dead. Not that I'd be the one killing them now, because I've got two babies and I've made a commitment of marriage to Kirk, but back then I totally would have gutted anyone who'd hurt Carly. I'm afraid…I'm afraid she's dead. Some nights I dream about her, and she tells me that she's okay, but I know she's not okay. Dead is not okay. Even when I'm eighty years old, I'll never stop thinking about her. I'll never stop praying for her and praying that whoever killed her suffers a horrible, horrible death. Might not be the most Christian thing in the world, but that's how I roll."

I saw a binky fly across the living room. A baby wailed.

Halley grinned. "I ate, and now it's their turns. If you don't mind viewing some side-boob or a nip-slip, then we can continue this conversation while the twins eat. If you're modest, then you can always swing by tomorrow with more enchiladas. I'm not modest, so don't worry about me. When you've got twins, any sense of propriety flies right out the window. It's all milk and poop right now. Milk and poop."

Milk and poop didn't sound appealing, but I'd seen enough women's bodies in my sixty-one years that watching someone nurse her babies didn't faze me at all, so I followed Halley back into the living room, sitting in the chair while she took the couch and deftly managed to nurse both babies at the same time.

"I know you'll think this is crazy, but I got into a true crime kick after Carly went missing," Halley announced.

"Books. Audiobooks. Podcasts. Those television shows. I think I was trying to make sense of it all. I'd met her parents and knew they were just as distraught over her disappearance as I was. Everyone at the Style Stable loved her. I went around to her other two jobs and talked to them, and they said she'd never had any problems with co-workers or customers. I knew it wasn't Memphis. For years I've been thinking that she had some stalker that she hadn't known about. It happens, you know. Some creep gets fixated on a pretty, lively, young woman and she has no idea she's the man's next target. You asked me what I think happened to Carly? That's what I think happened to her."

I glanced down at my notes, feeling overwhelmed. A random killer. Maybe this had been his only murder, or maybe not. Maybe he'd known her through one of her jobs, or the apartment complex she'd lived in, or maybe not. Maybe the killer had been one of Memphis's friends or just a random guy who'd seen her in a bar one night, or walking down the street. No wonder Carly's disappearance had become a cold case. There were just too many "could have beens."

"What were Carly's other jobs?" I asked, grasping at straws. The Style Stable had gone under two years ago, so it would take some digging to find Carly's co-workers from there, but maybe I could pluck some low-hanging-fruit from her other jobs.

"She did late shifts at Deanne's Diner in Beaver Falls," Halley told me. "And she worked every Friday, Saturday, and Sunday at McCray's Orchard."

CHAPTER 18

*M*cCray's Orchard.

Apples that the ghost kept pushing out of my fruit basket. The mark on the side of the box that Henry had found the skull in. And now, I'd just discovered that Carly Billings had worked at the orchard.

It couldn't be coincidence.

I was sure that lots of people bought fruit there as well as the cider, pies and jellies they sold, but it couldn't be a random occurrence that a skull was found in a box bearing that name, and the missing woman who might have been the victim had worked there. Was the murderer one of the owners? Another employee? A regular customer? What idiot would use a box from where he worked to store the skull of the co-worker he'd killed, under a bunch of decorations? Although if he never expected to get caught, maybe he'd done it because it was funny. I could imagine a psychopath finding such irony amusing.

All those thoughts ran on a loop through my mind as I drove to the orchard. McCray's was open for business, even though it was April and they had no fresh apples to sell. The front open-air section was empty, but I knew that come summer it would be full of bins and tables selling not only their apples and other fruits, but local vegetables as well. Inside the long narrow building was the retail side of the business. Jams, jellies, and preserves lined the back wall, along with an assortment of pickled vegetables. A huge refrigerated unit held gallons of various ciders. Other shelves held apple-themed salt-and-pepper shakers, shot glasses, and decorative items. Spinning displays near the register were filled with books and postcards. A bored young woman sat on a stool behind the register, reading a novel with the shirt-less torso of a man on the cover. I couldn't quite make out the book's name, but it looked like something I might like to read myself.

The cashier, a young woman with wispy, sandy-blonde hair, who appeared to be barely eighteen, looked up when I entered, smiled, then went back to her book. "Let me know if you need any help," she said, her tone expressing mild regret that her job was interfering with the plot of her novel.

I let her be for a moment while I explored the store. It had been ages since I'd in a roadside farm store. There were a whole lot more products available than I'd expected, but Molly had said the place was struggling, so expanding their products was probably a desperate attempt to bring in as much revenue as they could in the off season.

I grabbed a gallon of spiced cider, and eyed the other selections. I wasn't one for a lot of jams and preserves, but I picked up a sweet-and-hot pepper jelly, thinking it would be especially good with cream cheese on a bagel. I also couldn't resist grabbing a jar of Chow Chow.

Eli used to make fun of me for eating the stuff. Chow Chow was a Pennsylvania Dutch relish consisting of pickled vegetables. Wax beans, green beans, lima beans, butter beans, cauliflower, bell peppers, corn, carrots, celery, onion and cabbage as well as whatever else had ended up on the cutting board. Originally it was a way to use the scraps from canning season, and I adored the sweet-and-sour flavor of the relish. My mother had never been one for canning and pickling, but Nana had, and I had fond memories of helping chop vegetables in her steam-filled kitchen, the counter full of sterilized canning jars in rows like glass soldiers.

While at Nana's house, I'd eat Chow Chow on my burgers or hot dogs, but I especially loved it on a chunk of crusty French bread.

Would Judge Beck like it? I knew he'd try it. The judge was game for just about anything I put on his plate. He might have the same disgust for the relish as Eli had, but I was buying some. And if I was the only one who ate it, then so be it.

"Did you find everything you need?" The cashier smiled at me again, sliding a torn scrap of paper into her book as she set it aside.

"I did, but I was hoping I could talk to the owners or a manager." I pulled out a business card and slid it across to her. "Anyone who might have known Carly Billings when she worked here five years ago."

She frowned at my card, then frowned at me. "Who?"

"A young woman about your age worked here part-time five years ago," I explained. "She went missing back then, and we have reason to believe she was killed."

The woman's eyes widened. "Seriously? And what does any of this have to do with her job here? Do you think it was a co-worker that did her in? A customer?"

I lifted a shoulder. "I'm just going over everything—her friends, her family, her jobs."

The woman nodded, then grabbed the receiver off the old, rotary-dial phone beside the register. "Hey, Mom? Can you come out here? No, I don't need another break. There's someone here asking about a Carly who worked here five years ago."

She hung up the phone and looked over at me. "She'll be right out."

"Your parents own the orchard?" I asked.

She nodded. "My mom does."

"How long has your family owned McCray's Orchard?" I asked her.

She snorted. "We're McCrays. We've been here for five generations. The place nearly went belly-up a bunch of times. Granddad had to sell some land off last year to a developer to keep us afloat, but that's it. Things have been easier since then, but Mom still busts her butt, trying to turn things around."

"Your grandfather passed?" I asked, wondering if her mother would remember Carly. I did the math and figured the woman had probably been in her thirties or early forties when Carly worked here, so she should.

"No, Granddad's still hanging in there." The girl's face fell and she looked at her romance book with longing. "He had a stroke a couple of years ago. Mom and I moved in to take care of him. He's doing okay, but he needs help getting around, preparing meals, and cleaning the house."

My heart swelled with sympathy. I'd taken care of Eli for ten years after his accident, and I knew the amount of work that went into this sort of thing. "Just you and your mom?" I asked, knowing the answer really wasn't any of my business.

She nodded, giving her eyes a quick swipe with the back of her hand. "I don't know my dad. Mom says he was some jerk she had one night with and never saw again. It's okay. Some kids don't have decent parents at all, but I've got Mom and I've got Grandpa."

I did the math in my head. "And Grandma...?"

Her shoulders dropped, and she glanced again at the

novel. "She died when I was three. Car accident. I don't remember her, but I have lots of pictures that Mom and Grandpa saved."

"I'm so sorry." This family had seen its share of tragedy, but what family hadn't? A non-existent father. A grandmother who had died too soon. A grandfather who'd suffered a stroke. He couldn't have been that old—sixties, maybe seventy. That hit a little close to home given that I was sixty-one.

Plus, Eli had died of a stroke. That had been the official cause of death, although he'd had so many physical issues since his accident that if it hadn't been a stroke it would have eventually been something else. Still, I remembered that day, how I hadn't recognized the signs at first, how I'd been wracked with guilt at his passing. If only I'd noticed sooner that something wasn't right. If only I'd called 911 sooner.

If only that accident ten years before had never happened.

It was painful, imagining what our life would have been like if he hadn't been in that car crash. He would have continued to work insane hours at the hospital. I would have kept on with my journalist career. We would have had our parties in the backyard with friends, Eli at the barbeque and me serving drinks as we chatted. We would have continued to renovate the old Victorian we'd bought to a magnificent splendor. We would have taken the occasional vacation. Grown old together. Died of old age, retired and ancient in some home, holding hands as we breathed our last.

But clearly God and the universe had other plans.

There was no going back. And while I could mourn the future I'd never have and the husband I still loved, life had taken an abrupt turn to the left. And as breathless and disoriented as that turn had left me, I was getting my bearings once again.

Eli would have wanted me to live on. And he would have approved of Judge Beck.

Judge Beck. The thought of him, of our night together, brought a smile to my face. For the second time in my life, I was in love. And what I felt for the judge didn't conflict at all, didn't diminish one bit what I felt for Eli. It was possible to love two people, to have such deep and intense feelings for more than one person. I could mourn deeply, and love deeply, both at the same time.

And feel sympathy for this girl's grandfather, who was probably close to my age, who'd lost his wife about the same time as Eli's accident, and who was now facing a long recovery after a stroke.

The girl continued, not realizing I'd taken a mental segue into the near past. "I'm not taking on this albatross. Not now, and not when she's ready to retire. Mom keeps saying I need to prioritize family and history and tradition, but I'm not buying it. I don't want to spend my life tending to a bunch of fruit trees and making jellies. No way. I want to go as far away from this podunk town and this orchard as possible."

"It's a big world out there," I told her. "There are plenty of choices that aren't Locust Point."

I loved this town, but I got that not everyone might feel the same. Still, I hated to tell this young woman that the very things she was trying to escape here, she'd find in spades at most small towns. And if she was thinking big city, she'd be in for a real cultural shock having grown up in Locust Point. Milford was our idea of a big city, and it was nothing compared to Richmond, Philly, or especially New York or Chicago or LA.

A woman in her midforties came out of a back room. She wore jeans, a gray T-shirt, and a white lab-coat that was splattered with what I assumed was apple juice. Recognition tickled in the back of my mind and I tried to place where I'd seen her before.

Locust Point wasn't a large town. I might have run into her at the grocery store or one of the festivals, or just out walking one day. Still... I frowned, thinking that it had been recent that I'd seen her.

The woman smiled and straightened her glasses as she approached me, then held out her hand.

"I'm Amanda McCray. Elise said you had questions about Carly Billings?"

I shook her hand then handed her a business card, giving her a few seconds to look it over before I spoke. "I do. I was hoping you could tell me about her job here, who she worked with, and any details about the day she went missing if you can remember them."

"Elise, why don't you go in the back room and run the bottler." She watched her daughter leave then turned to me. "I don't know why I'm protecting her. The girl has her heart set on going to New York City this fall. She realizes that these things happen, but knowing that a woman, an employee, disappeared right here in a small town might bring it home to her how dangerous the world can be."

"I understand the urge to keep them innocent as long as you can," I told her.

"Well, maybe it's past the time for innocence." Amanda pulled a pair of stools out from behind the counter. "Here. Sit. And we'll talk about Carly. I don't know how much I can help, though. I told everything to the police five years ago when she went missing. I'm guessing her family hired you? Not that I blame them. If Elise went missing, I'd spend every last dime I had trying to find her. I'd never give up searching and hoping."

"Me either," I carefully skirted the question of who had

hired me, and asked once more for her to tell me about Carly.

"Really pretty girl," Amanda said. "But she didn't work it, you know? She knew she was good-looking, but she didn't flirt with the customers or the staff, or try to use her looks to gain any advantage. I got the feeling if a customer came on to her, she'd just ignore it and remain professional. Part of it might have been that she really loved her boyfriend. Not that he was worth it, in my opinion. The guy was one of those good-looking bad-boy types. Now *he* worked it. I think he liked the attention Carly gave him, but I think he would have dumped her in an instant if he found greener pastures, you know? I always thought he had something to do with her disappearance. When she didn't show up for her shift the next day, I'd just assumed she'd gone off with him. Everyone did."

I'd already gotten the scoop on the boyfriend, but wanted other information from Amanda.

"What about customers? Were there any who flirted with Carly? Any regulars who paid her a lot of attention? Any co-workers that might have been harboring a secret, or not-so-secret crush on her?"

Amanda shook her head. "No. I mean, some customers flirted. I could tell that a few of them thought she was attractive, but nobody took it too far. I make it very clear that there's a zero tolerance policy here on any sort of harassment. I don't care how much a customer spends, if he—or she—crosses the line, then they're out and banned. I've got a daughter, and I need to set an example for her that stuff like that is unacceptable. Any company that covers it up or asks their employees to just tolerate advances or lewd comments from customers isn't one people should work at."

I agreed, but sometimes a well-known policy like that just drove the bad actors to hide.

"Any complaints about strange cars in the parking lot or down the road, especially when employees were getting off work or you were closing the store?" I asked. "Even months before Carly went missing?"

Amanda frowned. "There was a van by the side of the road just south of the parking lot a month before she vanished. I only remember it because people were joking that it was a white van waiting to kidnap people. I sent my father out to check on it, and he said it had the hood open a few inches and a white rag tied around the antenna. No one was in it from what he could see."

"A broken down van," I mused. "How long was it there?"

She shrugged. "A few days, I think. One morning it was gone. No one came to the store to borrow our phone for a ride or to call Triple-A, but everyone has cell phones. We didn't recognize the van as belonging to an employee or a customer, but I didn't want to call the cops or have it towed. Some poor guy looking at a repair bill didn't need me adding to it with towing and impoundment. I've got the license number here if you want it. I gave it to the police as well five years ago. I'm guessing it wasn't important, since it doesn't seem like anything came of it."

She scrolled through her photos, wrote something down on a sticky pad on the counter, then passed it over. I glanced at it before slipping it into my purse.

"What about the day Carly went missing," I asked. "Did she work here that day?"

Amanda nodded. "It was a Saturday, which is our busiest day. All hands on deck, especially in September when everyone is buying apples and cider. She worked from noon until closing at seven. I was surprised when she didn't come in the next morning for work, but that sometimes happens with employees. And people said she was on the fence about leaving with her boyfriend, so I figured that's what she did.

I'd expected some kind of notice, but some people don't bother with that."

"Did anyone walk out with her? A co-worker getting off at the same time, or a manager escorting her to her car?"

"I can't remember if a co-worker left with her or not." Amanda frowned. "Probably not. Lots of them hang around to help clean or to chat. Carly never did because she always had another job to go to. The girl worked three jobs. I would have had dark circles under my eyes if I'd put in those sorts of hours, but she was always fresh and energetic even with a weird sleep schedule."

"So no one?" I pressed. "She just left on her own? Did you see her car pull out?"

Amanda held up her hands. "I can't say for sure that no one left at the same time she did. The police interviewed everyone, but I don't remember anyone saying they had. It was light out at seven in September, so we didn't worry about employees going out to their cars. We could see if there were other cars in the parking lot or not. We always have an employee working outside where we sell the fresh fruit and local vegetables. At seven they would have been putting things away and wheeling the bins inside to lock up. They would have seen if something had happened in the parking lot and raised the alarm. And they would have definitely heard it if Carly screamed or even called out. None of that happened, so I'm assuming she left without incident."

I made a quick note on my pad of paper. "Do you know who worked outside that day?"

"Five years ago?" Amanda shrugged. "I gave the police everything back then. Employee schedules, my statement, everything. Honestly, I can't remember who worked where back then. But I do know that whoever it was, they must have not seen anything, or they would have raised the alarm —or at least told the police about it. She vanished. She left work, took off somewhere, and never came back. And that's all I know."

I sighed, thinking that I'd hit a dead end here. "So, Carly's car was gone when you left that night?"

"Yes." Amanda hesitated. "Which again made me think she drove away without any problems. According to the police, she never made it to her night-shift job at Deanne's Diner. At first I thought she'd just run off with her boyfriend, but once the police got involved, I began to wonder if there had been someone hidden in the backseat waiting for her, or if she'd trusted someone enough to offer them a ride. I worried that she'd been carjacked, that they'd find her in a shallow grave somewhere. It still sends chills through me thinking what might have happened to her. My daughter is almost the same age as Carly when she went missing. There isn't a day I don't worry the same thing might happen to her."

I could only imagine. Once more I thought of Madison and how frantic I would be if this had been her. I don't think I ever would have given up searching, even after all hope was gone. I would have wanted to know what had happened. I would have wanted to know. And I would have wanted whoever had killed her brought to justice.

And Judge Beck... I shivered thinking of how he would react if Madison had vanished like this. He was a man of law, a man who put his faith in the system, but he would become a very different man if something had happened to his daughter. I could easily see him employing all of his resources, calling in all of his favors to track down the killer. And then delivering justice on his own, no matter what oaths and vows he'd taken. Family was family, and some things transcended the rule of law.

I wouldn't have blamed him one bit.

"Thank you so much for your time." I told Amanda as I

put my notepad and pen away. "If you think of anything else, please call me."

"I will. Are these your purchases?" She stood and went over to the register. "Good choice on the pepper jelly, by the way. It's one of my favorites."

Amanda rang everything up, convincing me to buy a box of four apple spice muffins as well. I normally liked to bake my own, but I'd been so busy with the charity yard sale and the skull that I hadn't had much time to cook. Plus I always liked to try other people's baked goods to get some ideas on how I might tweak my own recipes.

As I left I hoped the expanded product selections increased their sales and that McCray's Orchard survived another generation.

CHAPTER 19

*B*ack at work I dove into the fraud investigation, trying to make up for the rather extended lunch. I tried to focus, to knuckle down and get this assignment done, but it was hard. My mind kept returning to Carly Billings, the box with McCray's Orchard written on the side, to the skull.

It was ridiculous. I didn't even know for sure that the skull I'd found belonged to Carly. Not that I regretted investigating the woman's disappearance and probable death, but it didn't escape me that these could be two separate cases.

But the ghost in my kitchen, the one who kept rolling apples out of the basket—I really got the feeling that she was Carly Billings. And the emphasis on the apples told me that the orchard she'd worked at was key to her disappearance and murder. What had happened five years ago? I'd been so consumed with Eli and his medical care, that I barely remembered the story of this missing young woman. And that made me feel guilty. A woman had been snatched somewhere between her job at the orchard and her job at the diner, and vanished. Died. I hadn't had time to focus on her fate back then, but I needed to now.

"You know, this *is* like one of those true-crime books," Molly announced. "It's really scary to think a woman could just disappear like that, and five years later, no one has any idea what happened to her."

I spun around in her chair, knowing that Molly was just as obsessed with Carly Billings as I was.

She turned to face me. "It seems like most of the time when someone gets murdered it's the husband or boyfriend or ex or someone close to the victim. But there are these cases where some creep fixates on a woman. They're stealthy. They don't draw attention to themselves. They don't try to chat-up the woman, or make her feel uneasy in any way. They don't get caught lurking around her car or her house, or following her. They keep a distance, and the only time they're visible is if they have a good reason to be where they are. I wonder if that's what happened to Carly? If she caught some weirdo's eye. Just some psycho who saw her at the store or taking a walk, and decided she was his next victim."

"And he stalked her, but kept it stealthy. Like going into where she worked to buy an apple pie each week," I mused.

Molly nodded. "Maybe he'd stop in to buy a pie when she wasn't working. He's not there every time she's scheduled. So the stalking slips under the radar. And when he makes his move, no one thinks he could possibly be responsible."

I shivered. "Molly, you scare me sometimes."

"I scare myself sometimes." She bent closer to the computer. "Whoever it was, they were smart. Of course it didn't help that her parents and friends didn't realize she was missing until *days* later. I worked my mojo and got copies of the initial police report. The diner called Carly's cell phone when she didn't show up, but that was it. They didn't notify anyone, since they figured she'd just quit without notice."

"That's not exactly a random occurrence with jobs in the service industry," I commented.

She nodded. "I know. I'm not blaming them for that at all. They didn't have a reason to be alarmed when she didn't show up. She didn't come home that night after her shift was supposed to end, but her parents said she sometimes spent the night at her boyfriend's or a friend's house and didn't always check in. Again, no blame there. She was twenty, and it sounds like they all had weird work schedules and were coming and going from the apartment at all sorts of times. Her friends noticed she didn't text or call them back, but by the time they started to worry, it was three days later. Three days of not showing up to work, not showing up at home, not returning calls or messages from friends or family or her jobs."

"Did any of her friends call Memphis? The boyfriend," I elaborated as Molly gave me a quizzical look at the unfamiliar name.

"Neither the parents nor her friends had his number. Which I can see given that she was twenty. One of her friends managed to track the boyfriend's number down, but it took her a week and by then Carly's parents had filed a missing person's report."

"Did the friend call Memphis?" I asked.

Molly shrugged. "The initial police report didn't say. If they did, he probably didn't answer. I know I never answer when I don't recognize the phone number. If I did, I'd spend half my day fending off spam calls about replacement windows, my expired car warranty, or student loan refinancing."

I completely understood. "So he probably didn't answer, and didn't bother checking his voice mail."

"And if he did check his voice mail and heard someone was looking for Carly, he probably didn't bother to call him back," Molly said. "By then he was in Florida, and they'd split up, so why bother to return the call?"

"That makes sense," I agreed.

Molly continued. "So we're on day three and Carly's parents finally file a missing person's report after they called her jobs and the few of her friends whose numbers they knew. The police didn't take her disappearance seriously at first. Again, no real blame there. She wasn't a minor. Her boyfriend had left town and the cop who took down the initial report said both the parents and the friends he spoke to indicated that she may have left to go to Florida with her boyfriend. They expressed concern that she wasn't returning their calls, but no one worried about the boyfriend being violent. There was no mention of stalkers or jealous ex-boyfriends, or anything to send up red flags. So the police tracked down the boyfriend's number, called him, then asked the local cops in Florida to do a welfare check."

"But she wasn't with Memphis," I said, thinking through the timeline. "He claimed she decided not to go with him, that she stayed behind, that they'd broken up days before."

"He was still a person of interest until the police found the car and realized that he'd been out of state when someone would have ditched the car."

I nodded. "Miles said it was found up in Pennsylvania somewhere? Abandoned and bleached clean?"

Molly nodded. "It was parked in the back of a Walmart parking lot. Lots of people stay overnight there, or even do some extended car-camping if they're homeless, and the managers are super tolerant of that. Which is really nice, you know? I mean, it's hard for homeless people living out of their vehicles to find a safe place to sleep, and some of those Walmarts are twenty-four hour. Plus there are lights, and other people staying the night there, so it's safer than the shoulder of some back road. They don't get hassled by the police like they would if they were sleeping in a commuter lot since it's private property."

"What else did you find out about the car?" I asked, impatient and not as fully appreciative about Walmart's liberal overnight parking policies as I normally would have been.

"Eventually some of the long-termers got worried because they didn't see anyone coming and going from the car, and there weren't any window shades. They peeked in, didn't see any sleeping gear, and figured the car was abandoned. They were concerned about what might be in the trunk, so they told the manager at the Walmart and he called the police. When they ran the tags, the car came up as belonging to Carly Billings. And the missing person's report came up as well."

"A month. The car was there a month." I shook my head, wondering if the initial investigation would have gone any differently if the car had been discovered right after it had been dumped there.

Molly grimaced. "Yeah. I know. It looks like the car appeared in the Walmart parking lot around a day or two after Carly went missing. By the time the police were called, any footage from the parking lot security cameras was long gone, so they have no idea if a man or a woman dropped it off, or even the exact day or time. The other people staying in the parking lot weren't positive on the date or time, and none of them saw the car arrive."

"No evidence in the car," I muttered. "Nothing at all except that it serves as an alibi for Memphis."

At this point I as well as everyone else probably assumed Carly was dead. It wasn't just the skull or the ghost I kept seeing out of the corner of my eyes that made me believe that. She'd been gone five years without a trace. Unless someone was homeless and living completely off the grid, that was a difficult thing to do. Licenses got renewed.

People's IDs were run in routine traffic tops. She would have needed a job, a bank account, an apartment, and all those things left clear traces. Plus the fact that her car turned up abandoned, cleaned and bleached, suggested foul play as well.

I thought once more on how difficult it was to vanish in an age of technology. The same thing would be true for the killer, though. The killer would have needed to park the car somewhere for a day or two while he cleaned it. That would have been a span of time that someone may have seen him or the car. And the same with the actual abduction. Carly had left her job at the orchard, but never made it to the diner. Somewhere between the two places she'd vanished, and her killer would have wanted to do the deed in a place where he would have had a good chance of not being seen. A remote location without a lot of random passersby to notice a car, a young woman, and a murderer who most likely had a car of his own.

That didn't even get into considering a safe place to stash the car, or where to hide the body before the skull ended up in a box of Halloween decorations.

First things first. I pulled up a map on my computer, hit print, then gathered up some highlighters.

"What route do you think Carly would have taken to go from the orchard to her job at the diner? She was a hard worker, rarely missing a shift, so I'm sure she would have gone straight there rather than stop back at the apartment or to visit Memphis."

Molly pulled a map of her own up on her screen while I sat down with the printout and the highlighters. "Okay, obviously she'd start out on Route 16 if she was leaving the orchard. Then I'm thinking a left on Sage Grass Road to Route 2, then a right onto Crestville Street to Seventh?"

I nodded, marking the route in blue. "Or she could have

stayed on Route 2 to Pemberly Street, and then south on Seventh."

"Maybe. Except there's a school zone there and it's all residential so the speed limit's twenty-five. It's longer distance-wise to take Crestville, but she could go forty instead of twenty-five."

Good point, but I still marked the Pemberly route in pink, jotting a note at the top of the page.

"I can't think of any other route she'd take, unless she forgot her uniform and needed to swing by home and change, or if she needed to get gas," Molly continued. "She could have had her uniform already in her car to change at the diner, but I've had to make a quick detour to get gas before. Better to put some in the tank and be a little late to the diner, than be filling the tank after dark."

"I wonder where her apartment was?" I frowned at the map.

"I've got it." Molly read off an address. "I pulled it off her credit report and driver's license. She was still living with her parents at the time she disappeared."

"She was trying to save money." I marked a detoured route to Carly's home in yellow, and one to the nearest gas station in orange.

When exactly had her shift at the diner begun that night? Did she have time for a quick side trip? If not, then where was the most ideal spot for an abduction to take place? Assuming she had been abducted in between the orchard and the diner, that was. If someone had grabbed her in either of the parking lots, surely an employee or customer would have seen it, so she must have been grabbed on her way to the diner.

Snatching someone from a moving vehicle wasn't practical, but neither was grabbing her at a busy gas station or in the parking lot of the apartment complex which was in clear view of a busy residential road.

I frowned, imagining someone hunkered down and hiding in her back seat. But if he'd startled her while she was driving, I would have assumed she would have wrecked the car. I know I would have if a man had appeared from my backseat to threaten me. Wrecked my car and died of a heart attack, most likely.

"I ran a skip trace on her," Molly admitted. "She didn't have much on her social media accounts, which is kinda weird for a girl her age. Her credit report showed her jobs, her address at her parents' house, and a cell phone account. No credit cards. No rent or utilities bills. No car payment."

I'd already run the same reports, so there was no surprises in what Molly had found. Young people often had little debt, so their credit reports weren't that much help in tracking their movements.

"Any bank accounts?" I asked Molly, realizing I hadn't dug that far.

"She had a checking account. Average balance at the time she went missing was three hundred dollars. It was closed a year ago."

I assumed by her parents. It must have taken them years to have her declared dead and go through probate since I doubted Carly would have thought to have a will. Three hundred dollars. It wasn't a lot for a young woman who was trying to save up, hoping to make those dreams of college and a better future come true.

"Whoever grabbed her, it wasn't for the money," Molly added. "No sizable withdrawals were made around the time of her disappearance. And nothing was withdrawn after the day she vanished. There were a few automatic deposits from her places of employment, but that was it."

I'd already assumed money hadn't been a motive, but this confirmed it.

"Motive is something we'll think about later," I told Molly. "Right now I'm trying to figure out the scene of the crime. If you were a killer, where on these routes would be the best place to snatch someone? Somewhere you'd be reasonably sure you wouldn't be seen, or that if she screamed, she wouldn't be heard?"

Molly looked at my map and circled a few areas with her pen, numbering them. "Okay. Thinking like a killer here—which I'm totally not, I'll have you know."

"The thought never crossed my mind." I bit back a grin.

Molly made notes on a spare sheet of paper as she continued. "If she needed to go back to the apartment, she would have made a right onto Route 16. Half a mile down the road she would have turned onto 75, which has a lot of traffic. Then some busy streets to the apartment, and through town and out Route 2 to 7th and the diner. The only spots for a killer to accost her with any reasonable chance of non-detection would be the half-mile on 16 from the orchard, or the portion of 7th with the old milk-processing plant and the closed car lot. Snatching her in the apartment building would be problematic at that time of the evening with a lot of people home. Plus that half-mile section of Route 16 is in decent view of the orchard, so the woman packing up from the outside sales area might have seen. In my not-a-killer estimation, it's too risky. Same problem with the gas station theory."

"So she didn't go home or to get gas." I pointed to the map. "What about this?"

"Either travel option to the diner gives the killer a nice long section of Route 16 to make his move." Molly stabbed at the map with her pencil. "Here, here, and here is where I'm thinking based on what I remember. The orchard extends a mile and a half along the road, and these spots are the back end of some fields. There's nothing until the turnoff to Sage Grass Road. Actually, there's nothing on Sage Grass Road outside of a few small houses on two acre lots and hobby farms until you get to Beaver Falls."

"This is really good, Molly," I told her. "So these are your top three spots for the killer to strike?"

She nodded. "This section on Sage Grass, right before Sage Grass, and the area of Route 16 that would be out of view from the orchard store."

"The only problem with this is that Carly would be driving," I mused. "The speed limit is forty on that road, and there are no stop signs until she reaches Sage Grass Road."

"But there are reasons a woman might pull over and stop," she countered. "It was still light out when she left the orchard. I don't know whether she'd pull over for a stranger, but if someone she knew was on the shoulder with the hood up on their car, obviously having trouble, then I'm sure she'd stop to help. Or someone who had an animal that was clearly in distress."

"That's true." My heart lurched at the thought. If I saw someone standing on the shoulder with a dog or cat that looked like it needed help, that maybe had been hit by a car, I'd pull over even if it was dark.

Was that how the killer had gotten to Carly? Had he lured her into pulling over, relying on the very human need to help someone in distress? And had she been taken and quite possibly killed at one of these three spots, so close to the job she'd just left?

CHAPTER 20

*T*headed home from work, my mind full of thoughts. Just as I was pulling into the driveway, my cell phone beeped with a text. It was from the judge.

Put pork chops in oven. Ran out to take Cagney to the vet.

My breath caught, near panic at the thought that the pup had been hit by a car or had eaten something she shouldn't have while we were at work.

Everything okay? I texted, trying not to think the worst.

All good. Just a precaution. I'll tell you about it when I'm home.

I was somewhat relieved at that, but still a little concerned as I climbed the steps to my porch. There were several large boxes stacked up by the door. One look at the return address clued me in that they were the security cameras and other electronics that the judge had ordered after the garage had been broken into. At the time, I'd let him do whatever he needed to protect us, but now that I suspected the break-in was related to the skull, I no longer had mixed feelings about all the security stuff.

The skull wasn't in my possession, so there seemed little chance that we'd suffer any further vandalism or attempted robberies, but the thought that a murderer, or someone trying to cover up for a murderer, had been going through my garage? *That* was disturbing.

In my line of work, and given my knack of finding dead bodies, there *was* a chance we might be targeted again. And given the judge's line of work, that pretty much doubled the chance. I wasn't thrilled about cameras and motion detectors everywhere, but it probably was the right thing to do—especially with the judge's children in residence every other week.

I let Taco out for his evening stroll, then dragged the boxes inside, hoping that whoever the judge had hired to install and set all this up would be by in the next week or so. I'd just gotten rid of boxes cluttering up my house, and was longing for the time when I could once more walk unimpeded from the door to my kitchen.

Checking on the pork chops in the oven, I pulled some potatoes from the bin and got to work. By the time Taco was yowling at the door to be let in for dinner, I had potatoes, liberally spritzed with olive oil and sprinkled with Old Bay Seasoning, in the oven.

I got Taco situated with his half-diet, half-Happy Cat food, then pulled the apple cider, pepper jelly, and jar of Chow Chow from my bag. The cider went on the stove to warm, with some cinnamon sticks and cloves floating on the surface. That done, I put out some bagel chips with a smear of cream cheese and a dollop of pepper jelly on each. The Chow Chow I put in a bowl to serve with dinner. Hearing the judge's SUV pull into the drive, I pulled out a bottle of wine. By the time he came through the door, I had a glass ready for each of us.

He walked in carrying Cagney. I felt a stab of worry, but when he put the pup down, she danced off, seeming to be perfectly fine.

"What happened?" I handed him a glass of wine and gestured toward the bagel chips. "When you said you were taking Cagney to the vet, I'll admit I panicked a little."

"You're not the only one." He took the wine glass and blew out a breath. "Looking back, I kinda feel silly about all this, but I've never had a dog before and I was worried I'd done something to permanently hurt her."

"What?" My eyes widened, wondering if he'd fed Cagney chocolate or let her gnaw on some lily leaves during their walk or something.

"Last night I jogged with her," he announced dramatically.

I waited for a few seconds, assuming more was coming. When he remained silent, I finally responded. "And?"

"She's too young to go jogging," he explained. "Evidently it's not good on their growing joints and can cause long-lasting problems. I was talking to Judge Sanchez today, and mentioned our run last night and that I was going to make it a daily thing. He told me how bad it was to run with dogs that were under a year of age, and what might happen. I'd had no idea."

"I didn't know that either," I told him, grateful that Judge Sanchez had said something before Judge Beck had made this an exercise routine.

"I'm going to admit here that I overreacted. I called the vet and basically bullied them into squeezing Cagney in this evening. And when I got to the animal clinic, I was demanding X-rays and MRIs."

I reached out to put a hand on his shoulder, smoothing down his arm and holding his free hand—the one that wasn't gripping a wine glass. "Is she okay? What did the X-rays and MRI say?"

He laughed, shaking his head. "The vet talked me off the ceiling. He did some tests with Cagney and declared her perfectly fine. Evidently one three mile jog didn't cripple our dog, and the occasional short burst of speed won't hurt her. He advised me to wait on any daily jogging until she was at least six months old—ideally a year."

"So...no X-rays or MRIs needed?" I asked.

"Not unless she starts limping or she's reluctant to walk, or jump, or run around the yard. The doctor said she'd need to be sedated for the X-rays and MRIs and he didn't recommend anything that extreme unless she started showing signs of discomfort or lameness." The judge shook his head again. "I'm such a fool."

"You're not a fool." I thought of the boxes in the foyer. "You're someone who cares about his dog, about his children, about the people he loves. You thought Cagney might have been hurt and you were ready to move heaven and earth to get her medical attention and ensure she was okay. That's a hero, not a fool."

"Thank you." He leaned down and kissed me. "You always make me feel better."

I smiled, that sensation of giddy butterflies in my chest at his kiss. "You always make me feel better too."

He took a sip of wine, his eyes on mine. I was the one who stepped back, torn between wanting to let dinner burn and drag the judge upstairs, and letting the tension build until after dinner. I wasn't a teen, so the "letting tension build" impulse won.

"I've got appetizers," I motioned to the bagel chips. "And a weird side dish from my childhood that you might hate. I also have cider mulling on the stove, which we can enjoy with or without a splash of alcohol post-dinner."

"Dessert," he said with a slow smile that had me realizing he was thinking of something other than hot cider.

Now that was something to anticipate. But in the meantime...

"Here." I picked up one of the bagel chips and fed it to

him. "What do you think?" I asked after he'd had a moment to chew and swallow.

He slowly nodded. "I like it. What's on top of the cream cheese? It's a little sweet and a little spicy."

"Pepper jelly." I smiled, remembering the last time I'd had it. "It varies depending on what kind of peppers are added, but it should be a nice mixture of sweet and spice. Some people like theirs super hot, but I prefer it on the sweeter side."

"It's good." He grabbed another and popped it into his mouth. "Did you make this?"

"Heavens no." I laughed. "I haven't canned since I was a kid. I had to run by McCray's Orchard today and picked some up along with the cider and the other surprise."

"Hope the other surprise is as good as this." He snagged another one. "Why were you at McCray's? Heather used to take the kids there in the fall to get fresh apples, but I wouldn't think they'd have much available this time of year."

"No fresh produce, but evidently they have all sorts of products available all year round." I went on to tell him about the early-morning call I'd gotten from Henry, my visit with Halley, and how everything seemed to tie in to the orchard.

"You think someone who works at the orchard had something to do with her disappearance?" the judge asked.

I nodded. "Or a customer. Molly has this theory about a random psycho stalking her, but I think it might have been someone closer to her—someone she trusted. We looked at the routes she would have taken the night she vanished on her way to the diner, and think she might have been grabbed along Route 16 or on Sage Grass Road."

"Not far from the orchard," he mused. "She would have needed a good reason to pull over—especially if she was hurrying to her next job. I can't see her doing that for a stranger or someone she didn't trust."

"Exactly." I glanced at Cagney, who was ferociously trying to decapitate a stuffed squirrel. "Unless that stranger had an injured animal. But that seems like a lot to stage. I think it was someone she knew and had reason to trust."

"Someone who knew when she was getting off work," the judge pointed out. "Someone who knew the area, where to hide the body, where to hide the car."

"Exactly." I frowned. "They would have to have left before her. I didn't think to ask Amanda McCray that when I talked to her. What employees left right before Carly? What customers did? I don't think someone would have risked sitting on the side of Route 16 or Sage Grass Road for long. It's a pretty deserted stretch of road, but there would be a chance someone would see him there and at the very least take notice."

"I agree." The judge saluted me with his glass of wine.

"I'm going to go out tomorrow morning and drive the routes," I told him. "There's only so much Google Maps and memory can tell me. Actually seeing where the isolated spots are—the places not visible from houses or the orchard store —will help me narrow down where the crime might have occurred."

"And there's the whole thing about stashing Carly's vehicle." He frowned. "The killer wouldn't have wanted to leave it on the side of the road for long. If he could, he'd want to shove it into some bushes or down a ditch where it would be hidden as soon as dusk fell. Then he'd need to be confident that he could tow it up and drive it away unnoticed. He'd need to have access to the right equipment for that."

"So a tow truck, or a tractor, or a backhoe or something," I speculated.

"Or a large diesel truck," the judge added. "A friend pulled me out of a ditch a few years back when I slid off the road during a snowstorm. He had an F-350."

159

"So we're looking at someone who worked at the orchard, or was a customer there, or was close enough to Carly to know her schedule," I said. "And they had access to a tow truck, a tractor or other type of heavy equipment, or a big truck. That has to narrow it down a bit."

I thought about the orchard. They certainly had tractors and other types of farm equipment. Who had access to all of that aside from the owners? I assumed a place that size had hired help in the orchard as well as in the store.

The oven timer dinged, and we pushed thoughts of murder aside for those of dinner. The judge set the table while I got everything out of the oven and on platters. We ate in the dining room, oddly formal for just the two of us. It was romantic, with candles lit, the nice china and the silver on the table. The judge refilled our wine glasses, and I watched as he sampled the Chow Chow.

Newsflash—he wasn't a fan. Just like Eli, he found the whole cold, pickled mixed vegetables a strange and not particularly enticing side dish. He still ate every bit of what he'd spooned onto his plate, even though I protested that he didn't need to. I ate mine as well, but enjoyed it with all the memories of childhood attached to the odd dish.

After dinner we both did the dishes and put away the food. Then the judge took Cagney out for a quick walk around the block while I put on some music and got our hot ciders ready. Even though we'd split a bottle of wine, I decided to indulge and added some caramel vodka into our ciders.

When he got back we curled up on the couch next to each other, listening to Earth, Wind, and Fire. Cagney lay at our feet, snoring lightly. Taco found a perch on the back of the sofa, his purr rumbling in our ears.

I leaned my head against the judge's shoulder. His arm came around my waist and snugged me close. We sipped our cider, letting our bodies melt together. His hand stroked my waist and I closed my eyes, falling into this moment here with him.

And when the needle lifted off the record, we went upstairs to bed. Together.

CHAPTER 21

*T*he next morning I was the one who left home early. Instead of heading straight to work, I took a detour to Deanne's Diner.

A cheery orange neon sign proclaimed them to be open and there were quite a few cars in the parking lot. I wasn't there for breakfast, though. Making a U-turn in their parking lot, I set the stopwatch on my phone and turned left.

This first trip I took the Crestville Street route, obeying every speed limit sign. The moment I pulled into the parking lot of the still-closed McCray's Orchard, I hit stop on my phone and jotted down that it had taken me twelve minutes and thirty-seven seconds.

The trip back I took the Pemberly Street route, and noted that it took fifteen minutes and six seconds. Then I did both routes once more, this time speeding, although not so fast that I was in danger of getting a ticket. Driving faster managed to shave under a minute off both times, but I could imagine a young woman worried about making it to her shift on time would be putting some pedal to the metal. One minute could make the difference between a scolding and losing a job at some businesses.

I drove both routes once more, slowing to an agonizingly slow speed as I hit the isolated stretch of Sage Grass Road and along Route 16. Sage Grass was bordered on both sides by wide open fields. There was no shoulder on the road, so anyone who pulled over would need to be right up against the crops on one side, and a foot into the road on the other. This time of year, the fields were turned dirt, smelling faintly of fertilizer and manure. I didn't know if these farmers planted corn or soy, but either way I couldn't see that this would be a good place to leave a car, or even to hide one. The vehicle would be dangerously in the road if the killer had left it up against the plowed field. And it would have been clearly visible in a field of soy. Corn might have hidden the car, but the destruction of plants that resulted from Carly's vehicle being pushed off the road would have been noticed by any passerby. It also would have been noticed by the farmer who would have most likely called the police to report the damage and complain.

Heading along Route 16, I saw a much different landscape. The road was slightly raised above the fields on either side. There was also a significant ditch before the ground rose to the farmland. On the left, there were patches of briars and weeds blocking the view of a plowed field. On the right, a similar thicket of briars and weeds clogged the wide and deep ditch, but they weren't tall enough to hide the rows of fruit trees in the acres beyond.

I pulled over onto the narrow shoulder and looked up and down the road. Nothing was visible from here—not the orchard store, not the farmhouses, not even the distant Sage Grass Road intersection. I hadn't seen one car since I'd been up and down here. And I could imagine how a vehicle could be hidden down the ditch, the approaching dusk and the briars and weeds keeping it from being seen except for all of the most eagle eyes.

Walking up and down the shoulder, I looked in the gravel, in the weeds, doing everything but actually climbing down into the ditch. Nothing was there, but I didn't really expect to find anything. It had been five years since Carly Billings had vanished, and a killer who'd had the foresight to clean and bleach her car before dumping it surely would have diligently searched this area, probably even running a metal detector over it all.

Even without a dropped bracelet, a small broken piece of bumper, or a torn scrap of clothing, I still knew I'd found the abduction spot—quite possibly the murder spot.

Sending J.T. and Molly a quick text telling them I'd be even later than I'd originally expected, I drove back to the diner lot, and this time I parked.

A woman with her dark hair in a high ponytail smiled as I walked in. "Just one, or is someone joining you this morning?"

"I'm not having breakfast today," I quickly said as she moved to grab a menu. "I wanted to get a dozen cinnamon rolls to go, and ask a few questions."

"About employment? We're always hiring." She put the menu down and pulled an application out from behind the hostess station. "Are you looking for early, afternoon, or evening shifts?"

"Actually I'm looking into the disappearance of someone five years ago." I handed her my card. "She used to work here. The late shift, I believe. When does that shift start?"

"Evening shift starts at seven, but I know the manager is sometimes willing to be a little flexible. It's so hard to get employees—especially ones who actually show up. We close at midnight, so it's a five-hour shift. Not as good money as breakfasts, but it's a nice side income for people with a day job.

I nodded, knowing that turnover was a real problem in retail and food service. I'd done my fair share of waitressing in college, and had found the job to be hard work for what was often minimal pay, so I couldn't exactly blame employees for bailing when they found something better.

"Is there anyone here now who might have been working five years ago and known Carly Billings?" I asked.

The woman frowned. "I've only been here six months, but let me get Bridget. She's the manager, and she might know."

The dark-haired woman left, and a few moments later returned with my cinnamon rolls and a second woman—this one with her coppery hair in a neat bun and thick-framed glasses perched on top of her head.

"Hi, I'm Bridget Vin." She shook my hand then motioned for me to follow her to a set of benches by the door, where patrons could sit while waiting for a table. "You wanted to know about Carly Billings?" she asked once we were seated.

I nodded, handing her a card. "Is there anyone around that was here when she worked at the diner five years ago?"

She barked out a sharp laugh. "That would be me, although I wasn't the manager back then. I'm the one that got her the job here, and when I found out she didn't show up that night, I was furious. I thought she'd run off with her boyfriend without any notice and that it would look badly on me for recommending her. I felt horrible when the news came out that she was actually missing."

"You were a waitress here at the time?" I asked, pulling out my notepad and pen.

"Yes. I worked the morning shift Monday through Friday. In the summers and in the fall, I worked weekends at McCray's for some extra money. That's how I met Carly. She was a nice girl, a hard worker. We weren't really friends or anything, but I knew her family had been in a real bad spot financially, and that she was busting tail trying to just make ends meet. I think she had plans of going to nursing school or something."

"But you immediately assumed she ran off with her boyfriend when she left with no notice?" I asked.

Bridget nodded. "He was one of those gorgeous bad-boy types. She wouldn't be the first girl to ditch her future plans for a hot guy. I mean, she seemed sensible, and I always thought she'd leave him if she got a scholarship or a windfall, but what do I know? Scholarships and windfalls are like winning big on scratch-off lottery tickets, and sometimes common sense flies out the window when a hottie is right there, twisting you up in knots with a sexy look."

I smiled sympathetically, noting the faint bitterness in Bridget's voice. "Was there anyone who paid a lot of attention to Carly that you know of? Anyone here or at the orchard? A customer or a co-worker, maybe?"

She shook her head. "The police asked me the same thing. She was a pretty girl, and nice, but she wasn't flirty or anything. And I didn't think that boyfriend of hers was particularly jealous. He wasn't always checking up on her, calling or texting her, or acting possessive like some guys do."

I scribbled down a few notes, trying to think of what else I might ask her.

"You know, I was working at the orchard the night she vanished," Bridget volunteered. "They closed at seven, and everyone else stuck around to clean up, but Carly always left early to rush here, so she wouldn't be more than ten minutes or so late for her shift. I worked the outside section of the store where all the fresh vegetables are sold, so I was always one of the last to leave."

I blinked, surprised to have run into one of the last people who had seen Carly before she vanished.

"Did her car start okay? Were there any problems you noticed her having? Anyone lingering around the parking area near her car?" I asked.

Bridget shook her head. "Her car started right up. She didn't exactly squeal wheels or anything leaving the parking lot, but she was clearly in a rush. And there was no one near her in the parking lot. I told the police that no one else left right after her. They wanted to know exactly who left next, and when. Two customers wrapped up their post-closing purchases, leaving right around the same time as Carly, but they went the other direction, toward the main road. I was busy counting out the cash drawer and wheeling the display bins back inside, but I don't remember there being any other customers after those two. Employees started leaving about quarter after seven, but by then Carly should have been either at the diner or close to it. Like I told the cops, most employees turn the other way out of the parking lot to get to the main road. No one's got any reason to make a left and travel all those back roads unless they're heading to the diner, those farms, or taking the scenic route around and back to town. And trust me, people getting off work at seven in the evening aren't looking to take the scenic route home."

I made an affirmative noise, thinking that I'd be eager to get back home as well.

Then I remembered that we'd all conjectured that Carly most likely stopped to help someone, rather than being followed from work and accosted while driving.

"What about...what about before Carly left?" I asked. "Who left before she did?"

Bridget frowned. "I really don't know. I'm sure there were a lot of customers who left right before closing. None of the employees. Well, except for Mr. McCray. He liked to collect extra money from the tills throughout the day, then run the deposit in to the bank before closing. Whatever was left at closing got accounted for, then put in the safe for the next day."

"When did Mr. McCray usually leave?"

"Maybe quarter 'til seven? Ten of?" She looked off into the distance, clearly trying to remember.

"And he'd be back in time to close the store?" I tried to make the events fit the timeline, but it seemed a bit tight. If the guy left at ten of seven, waited at the side of the road for Carly, abducted or killed her and stashed the car, would he have time to be back by fifteen or twenty after to close the store? I couldn't imagine so.

"No, he didn't usually close up for the night," Bridget said. "At least, he was never back by the time I left. The woman who managed the place usually locked up. I think her name was Alice."

"Amanda?" I asked, assuming that the elder McCray would have his daughter managing the store. "Amanda McCray?"

"Oh no." Bridget chuckled. "I remember Amanda. She was in charge of the actual orchard. She'd take care of the trees, manage the harvest, sort through the apples so that the pretty ones went for sale and the scratch-and-dents went into the cider room. That woman worked some insane hours —and her a single-mom with a little kid too. She managed the farming end of things, managed the cider presses, and the jams and jelly production. I think they outsourced the pies and baked goods, but everything else she handled. I always felt a bit sorry for her. The woman had no life besides the orchard."

"So Alice would lock up the store, and Mr. McCray might or might not have returned after the bank drop," I mused, getting back to the first decent suspect I'd had in this case. "What can you tell me about Mr. McCray? What was he like?"

She smiled fondly. "Such a nice man. He was so sweet and kind. Never a harsh word. Never got flustered when we were busy or when customers got mad about something. I think it used to drive Amanda a bit crazy, but I don't blame her. She worked her rear off and her father putted around the store, chatting with employees and customers. Plus I got the impression that they weren't making a lot of money and that the orchard might have been in some financial trouble. They were busy, but there was a lot of overhead and employee cost, and they didn't get quite as much traffic as the roadside stands right on the busier streets."

He didn't sound much like a killer, but true crime stories were filled with murderers that their neighbors and co-workers described as "such a nice guy."

"Was he particularly friendly with Carly?" I pressed.

Her eyebrows went up. "Yeah, but not like you're thinking. I mean, I think he felt sorry for her knowing that her family was so poor and that she wanted to go into nursing school. He'd talk with her, but he was never inappropriate. He'd eat here at the diner pretty regularly, and I heard when he came in during the evenings, he'd ask to sit at Carly's table and tip her really well. But it wasn't creepy or gross or anything. He wasn't that kind of man. I got the impression he was really lonely since his wife died and Amanda worked all the time. Plus Amanda and her daughter didn't live with him. Maybe Carly reminded him of his daughter or granddaughter. He was just a nice, lonely guy."

"Uh-huh." Nice lonely guys fell in love too, and maybe they weren't so nice if the object of their affection didn't reciprocate their feelings. Or decided to leave town with her sexy boyfriend.

"People thought it was the boyfriend that killed her," Bridget added. "They think she refused to leave with him, and he murdered her and stashed her body, then took off. I don't believe it thought. He showed up at the orchard a couple of times and just didn't seem like the hot-headed type. And he had a roving eye, if you know what I mean. I could see a girlfriend popping *him* for sleeping around, but I couldn't imagine him getting upset enough to kill Carly. I think he'd just shrug and leave if she decided not to go—leave and never look back."

That was pretty much what Hally had said as well.

"Who do you think killed her?" I asked Bridget as I got out the money for the cinnamon rolls.

She held up her hands. "I think maybe it was an accident. Like a drunk ran her off the road, she died, he panicked and buried her somewhere and ditched her car."

If that was the case, then we might never find out who killed Carly. Except for the skull—that might be the one piece that could link the killer to the crime. Once the DNA results were in, once Keeler tracked down who had donated the box with the skull in it, then even an accidental killer might find himself finally paying for his crime.

CHAPTER 22

*E*arly that morning I'd gotten a text from Bert Peter asking me to swing by and pick up his list of donors as well as a few antiques he wanted Henry to research for him, so I drove there from the diner, feeling a twinge of guilt at how very late I was going to be going in to work today.

But the guilt was short-lived. J.T. had given this "investigation" his blessing, wanting new material for his YouTube channel, and I could always do some work in the evening after the judge and I had dinner.

Turning into the development, I admired the rows of well-kept bungalows and Cape Cod houses. The dwellings might be fifty years old, but it was clear that the homeowners cared about curb appeal. No deferred maintenance here. I'd never been to Bert's house before, but I was struck by the stark difference between his cedar-sided two-story home and the big Victorian he'd inherited when his uncle, Harry Peter, had passed.

Henry had been going over to Harry Peter's house across the street since he'd died, helping Bert go through the yard and house full of junk. At first, Bert paid Henry to help him sort through boxes, toss things into a dumpster, and do some general cleaning, but he'd quickly discovered the boy had an eye for collectables and antiques. After Henry had turned what he'd thought was junk into cold hard cash, Bert decided to add a commission to Henry's pay.

It was bittersweet that Bert had finalized things with his uncle's estate and the house and was ready to put it on the market. As excited as I was to have new neighbors, I'd miss Bert. Hopefully he'd keep in touch and come over for the occasional Friday happy hour on my porch.

I wasn't the only one who would miss him. He and Henry had become friends, and I knew Henry loved researching the various items Bert gave him from the house, as well as recommending prices and where to list them for sale. I'd need to talk to Judge Beck and see if we couldn't get Henry a job this summer at one of the antique shops, or even with an auctioneer. The boy was only fourteen, but surely there was something he could do that would feed his interest in antiques and history.

It was late on a Wednesday morning, but judging from the cars in the driveway as well as the people out and about in front of their houses, this neighborhood had quite a few retirees, stay-at-home parents, and work-from-home folks. Quite a few waved at me as I drove by, even though I clearly wasn't recognized as living here.

Bert was outside, mulching under the hedges that lined the front of his tidy brick ranch-style home. I pulled into the driveway, and waved as I got out, noting once more that he wasn't the only one taking advantage of the nice weather to do a little yard work. Two other neighbors were weeding, and edging their walkways, and a man a little older than me sat on his porch, watching the birds at his feeder.

Bert wiped the dirt from his hands, and picked up a box

from his porch, carrying it to my car. I popped the trunk, not at all bothered that he obviously wasn't going to invite me in or ask me to linger. I needed to get to work sometime this morning, and Bert was clearly busy, putting in the work to make his front garden magazine-worthy.

He settled the box in my trunk. "There's a clock in here that's probably junk, but this mid-century stuff is sometimes collectable so I want to get Henry's opinion on it. There's also a glass bowl, and a vase I'd like him to check out as well."

I nodded. "He won't be back until Sunday night. While he might be able to do a little research early next week, it's going to depend on homework and after-school sports."

Bert shrugged, sending a quick smile my way. "School-work, commitments, and family come first. These things aren't going anywhere, so there's no rush. I just wanted to know if I needed to add their value to the estate paperwork or not."

He pulled a sheet of paper out of the box and handed it to me. "And here's the list. I walked down the street and around the neighboring blocks to help me remember which houses I got donations from. I'm pretty certain about the number of boxes, sizes, and a few items, so I put those there as well. If I knew the homeowners, I put their name down, but a lot of them I didn't even get their first names. Isn't that sad? When I was a kid, I knew every neighbor's name in a three block radius—well, their last name, kids' names, and pets' names, anyway. Now that I'm an adult, I'm lucky if I know a dozen people on my own street."

I smiled in agreement, glancing down at the list. "Oh, me too, although a dozen is more than most people know, I'll bet. It helps that in my neighborhood, we haven't had a lot of houses bought and sold in the last few years. And the Friday happy hours help too. You should do some neighborhood events now that you're wrapping up things with your uncle's estate. It would be a good way to get to know everyone."

"It might be a good idea this summer," he agreed. "Maybe a big barbeque or something. I'll make sure to invite you."

"Oh, I'd love—" I frowned at the list. "McCray? Glen McCray?"

"Yeah." He pointed across the street to where the man sat on his porch watching birds. "That's Glen. Although it wasn't him that gave me the boxes, but his granddaughter. I think her name is Ellen or Elaine or something. Glen had a stroke a few years ago. He's recovered mostly, but still has some issues where he really can't drive or work anymore. His daughter and granddaughter moved in with him right after the stroke to help him out. Poor guy. He's only in his midsixties. Really tragic to have a stroke at that age."

"Elise? Daughter is Amanda? They own McCray's Orchard?" I asked, remembering that Elise had said her grandfather had suffered a stroke. It couldn't be a coincidence. They had to be the same family.

"That's them. I remember the orchard fell on some hard times a couple of years ago. Thought they would have to sell it, but the daughter managed to turn things around somehow. She runs everything now. Thank goodness they're close, because this stroke of Glen's came out of the blue. She seems really devoted to him. And to her daughter."

A chill crept over me. The skull. The box. The apple rolling across my kitchen island.

"Do you know Glen? What kind of person is he? His wife died about ten or eleven years ago, didn't she?"

Bert nodded. "That was real tragic. Glen took it hard. He's a good guy. Easygoing. Friendly. Kind. I go over and visit every now and then when I see him on the porch. Poor guy is so lonely. His daughter works crazy hours, and the granddaughter isn't around much. I think he misses his wife a lot. I feel bad for him."

I felt a twinge of sympathy myself, but "nice, lonely guy" didn't mean Glen McCray wasn't a murderer.

"How long have you known him? His wife? His daughter and granddaughter?" I asked, trying to do the math in my head.

"I bought this place right before Glen's wife died. Really nice woman. She brought me an apple pie the day I moved in, and boy was it good! I'm not sure if she made the pies and muffins for the orchard store or not, but she was quite the baker. Her death was a real shock—car accident. Like I said, Glen was wrecked. I barely saw him the rest of that year."

I blinked away tears, thinking of Eli's accident and how it had rocked my world. I'd sat beside his hospital bed, alternately praying and cursing a cruel fate that would let this happen to the man I loved. Had Carly resembled his lost wife? Had he snapped when she hadn't returned his affection, unable to lose someone he loved once more? It sounded farfetched, but grief and loneliness did things to a person's heart and mind. And everything fit—the apple, the box, the orchard, and the man sitting on his porch right across the street.

"I wasn't living here when the granddaughter was born," Bert continued, "but I remember neighbors telling me it was a real scandal. The father was some jerk who ran off when the daughter got pregnant. Glen and Carol stepped up to the plate and supported her. She took on a major role in the business, and Carol watched the baby. They both loved the baby, and did all they could to make sure their daughter didn't suffer because the father of her kid was a loser."

Glen really didn't sound like a killer, but then again, some killers were good at fooling people. "Does he have any hobbies? Did he socialize with the neighbors much?"

"I heard he and Carol used to play bridge with a neigh-borhood group. And I know they were very active with Meals on Wheels, delivering food to elderly shut-ins. If there was a neighborhood event, one of them participated, but after she died, Glen was kinda lost. He spent a lot of time at the orchard, I guess. I really didn't see him much until after the stroke." Bert rubbed his chin in thought for a few seconds. "Honestly, that's about it."

I looked over at the house and the man. "I guess I just assumed there was a farmhouse or something on the orchard property. I wouldn't have expected the owners to be living in a development."

"I think at one time the orchard was part of a larger farm, but it got sold off separately from the rest of the farm," Bert said. "I'm not sure if it was in their family back then or not. Maybe someone at the Historical Society would know."

"And you have no idea what they donated?" I asked, glancing once more at the paper.

Bert held up his hands. "Three boxes. The granddaughter said they were up in the attic, that she had been going through stuff up there in her spare time, trying to make some space. She was hoping to have a little studio or private area up there, I think. I remember her mentioning it was holiday decorations and some dishes, but I didn't look through them. The one box was kinda heavy but the other two weren't. They were all boxes from the orchard though, with the logo and McCray's Orchard stamped on them. I remember that."

The orchard. The boxes. The apples. Glen *had* to be the killer. If Elise was going through stuff in the attic, then I doubted she would have given away one of the boxes she and her mother had brought with them when they moved in. No, she would have given away what a quick glance had told her was old decorations and dishes that were just taking up space

—stuff that was there when they'd moved in to help her grandfather after his stroke.

Elise obviously hadn't known what was in the boxes, and normally I would have doubted Amanda had either, but piecing it all together, I suddenly remembered where I'd seen the woman before. She'd been at the charity yard sale, asking about holiday decorations—especially Halloween decorations. She'd said that she'd just moved into a new house and wanted some inexpensive items to do it up big for the holidays.

Once again, it seemed like too much of a coincidence. Why would she want to buy used decorations for her father's house, when they probably had plenty of their own? Why would she be thinking about Halloween and Christmas this time of year when she had a father who needed help, a teetering business to keep afloat, and a teen daughter who wanted nothing more than to leave town and the family business?

Amanda knew. Maybe she didn't know at first. Maybe Elise had mentioned giving away the boxes, then Glen had confessed to his daughter what was in one, and she'd come to the yard sale desperate to buy the skull back before someone noticed it was real.

Or maybe she'd known all along.

Either way, she'd spoken to me yesterday about Carly Billings, and the whole time she had to have known her father had killed the girl. She'd known while answering my questions. And my garage break in, and Bert's attempted break in of his car. Suddenly that all made sense.

Glen McCray had murdered Carly Billings five years ago. I wasn't sure what his motive was, but I was positive he'd done it. And now his daughter was an accessory after the fact.

I knew this, but I couldn't prove it. All I had was a bunch

of circumstantial evidence that could have been coincidence. All I had to go on was a bunch of associations, and the clues left by a ghost.

None of that would hold up in court. And none of that was enough for Detective Keeler to be able to make an arrest.

CHAPTER 23

I pulled over to the side of the road as soon as I was out of Bert's development, and called Keeler. This time I got his answering machine instead of Toots, so at least I was sure he'd get the message.

I told him what Bert had said about the orchard logo on the boxes, and that he'd been told at least one of the boxes had holiday decorations. That these donations were from the McCray house. Then I snapped pictures of the list Bert gave me and e-mailed it to the detective from my phone along with my very long list of theories. I told him about my interviews with Hally, Amanda, and Bridget, about driving the routes between the orchard and the diner, and that in spite of everyone's label of "nice guy" that I suspected Glen McCray had murdered Carly Billings five years ago, and that it was her skull I'd found in that box.

I knew he'd probably be rolling his eyes as he read my message—either that or cursing me for interfering in an active investigation. Maybe both.

During the drive to the office, I went over the timeline in

my mind, trying to figure out how Glen had done it, and how the skull had ended up in a box in his attic.

Carly had left work at seven, although Amanda might have been lying about that, Bridget had corroborated it. She'd driven out of the orchard parking lot, but never made it to her job at the diner. Somewhere along the stretch of Route 16, she'd encountered her killer.

Glen had left fifteen minutes early as usual, supposedly on a run to the bank with the deposit, but if he had turned left out of the parking lot instead of right, no one might have noticed. Had Glen he pulled over, pretended to have a break down, and then confronted Carly about her feelings? About her possible decision to leave for Florida with Memphis? Her friend Hally had said that Carly hadn't mentioned anyone stalking her, or being nervous or anxious about anyone. If the owner of the orchard where she worked had been on the shoulder supposedly with car trouble, she most likely wouldn't have been at all suspicious. And a nice woman who trusted her kindly employer wouldn't have thought twice before pulling over to help—even if it meant she'd be extra late to her next job.

But then what? I'd gone through all the theories, bounced ideas off Molly, J.T. and the judge. Knowing the isolation of that road, the scant traffic there, and the fact that the first half mile of the road bordered the orchard property, I was willing to bet Glen McCray had incapacitated Carly, put her in his car, then pushed her car off the road where it would be hidden from view until he could dispose of it later.

Her car was found a month later in the Walmart lot in Pennsylvania up near York, and from what Molly said, the police report indicated it had been there for three to four weeks. Glen must have moved the car soon after abducting and killing Carly.

Although he might have been confident enough to leave it there for at least a few days. Down in the ditch and hidden by brush, it wouldn't have been easy to spot. And if it had been found, then someone might have assumed that someone had an accident and ran off the road. At that time, Carly's disappearance wasn't even considered to be because of foul play. Even if it had been, suspicion wouldn't have turned toward her employers.

I was sure that was what happened, but I had no real proof. And I still didn't know where Glen had hidden her body or why her skull had ended up in a box of decorations in his attic. I couldn't believe he would risk taking her back to his house in a development where very nosy neighbors would have seen him smuggling a body into his house, or burying one in his backyard.

He'd probably buried her at the orchard, I thought. The orchard was a hundred acres of fruit trees and bushes. He had farm equipment. Compost and mulch piles. Outbuildings. No one would have thought twice about him digging holes in a remote part of his orchard.

Except...Amanda was managing the farm portion of the business. She would have noticed if her father, who normally only ran the store, was out after dark using the equipment to dig holes in the orchard. Even if she hadn't seen him in the act, she would have noticed the turned-over ground, and mentioned it to him before she made any sort of official report.

Had he told her then what he'd done? Had she agreed to keep it quiet, to protect her family and the business that was her and her daughter's sole livelihood? Amanda was a hard worker, dedicated to the family. She was a single mom with limited employable skills outside her family business. She and her daughter relied on the orchard. She couldn't afford to let her father's unfortunate mistake ruin their finances, ruin hers and her daughter's futures.

And when Elise accidently gave away a box from the attic that contained Carly's skull, Amanda jumped in to correct the situation.

But why *was* the skull in a box in the attic?

I didn't know that. And I really didn't want to dwell too much on what might have happened to Carly after Glen had abducted her. Doctor Basava had said the skull appeared to have been buried in a shallow grave before it was excavated. Whatever had happened to Carly, I was pretty sure her body had ended up somewhere in the orchard. And for some reason, she'd needed to be moved, and the safest place to put her remains had been in boxes in the attic.

Two or three years ago Glen had suffered a stroke. I seriously doubted the body had been moved before that, which meant that Amanda had once again jumped in to help her father, moving the body and keeping the family secret. As much as I sympathized with the woman, she was just as guilty as her father. There was a family in Locust Point who needed closure, who needed to know what happened to their daughter—and wanted a killer to be brought to justice. Glen was a killer, but his daughter was equally to blame.

I parked in the lot, grabbing the cinnamon rolls off the seat before I went into the office. J.T. was just hanging up from a phone call and Molly was hunched over her computer as she worked.

Molly smiled up at me, her eyes straying to the box in my hand.

"Cinnamon rolls," I said as I held them up. "From Deanne's Diner."

"I've never eaten at Deanne's Diner, but I'm not saying no to a cinnamon roll." She hopped up from her chair and went to the coffee station, refilling her mug and grabbing a pastry from the box. "So tell me what you learned. I deserve a break after slaving away here by myself for hours."

"Yes, tell us what you learned." J.T.'s eyes gleamed and I could tell he was already casting roles in his next video.

I got a cinnamon roll and some coffee for myself, sat down, and told them everything I'd discovered this morning.

"Glen McCray?" Molly's eyes were wide. "Isn't he...like ancient or something?"

I winced. "He's midsixties. Not that much older than I am."

"Well, you definitely seem younger," Molly quickly tried to cover up her misstep. "He's a grandpa. And didn't you say he'd had a stroke?"

"He did have a stroke a couple of years ago," I said. "He's young for that sort of thing, but it happens. My husband Eli died of a stroke."

Molly winced. "I'm so sorry. I didn't mean any disrespect, Kay. You just seem more like my mom's age to me."

Because I didn't have children or grandchildren? Because I was dating a younger man? I pushed those thoughts away, refusing to take offense. I was sixty-one, and that was young in my mind. There were plenty of unfortunate people my age and younger that had health concerns that limited them, but thankfully I was not one of those people. And I chose to believe that was what Molly had meant by her comment.

"Do either of you know Glen McCray?" I asked both of them.

Molly shook her head. "Nope. I've been to the orchard but maybe once or twice in the last few years, and I don't remember seeing anyone besides the younger people who're working the cash register. It's creepy to think that Carly's boss, some old guy, would just grab her like that. And kill her."

"First, he's not much older than I am," I pointed out, still stinging about the whole age thing. "And he was my age when Carly went missing. I'm dating a younger guy. It's not that weird, especially for an older man and a younger woman."

"Judge Beck is maybe ten years younger than you," J.T. pointed out. "Carly would have been young enough to be Glen's granddaughter."

Judge Beck was almost fifteen years younger than me, and it still occasionally bothered me. Not when we were alone together or with the kids or friends, but when we were out in public. I worried that people might see us and wonder what the heck a young, attractive, successful man like him saw in me. I worried that they were labeling me as some sort of cougar, and thinking this was a passing fling for a man who'd just seen the end of a long marriage.

There were times I had the same thoughts. Then I realized that life needed to be accepted as it came. Judge Beck was not the sort of man to indulge in a frivolous affair—especially with someone who owned the home he lived in, who was close to his children. We were friends. And I knew he would never jeopardize that friendship for a quick toss in the sheets.

And we'd hardly had a quick toss in the sheets. For Pete's sake, it had taken us eight months to express interest in each other and longer to even kiss. We'd been dating for two months before we'd even made it into the bedroom. It reassured me that these were not the actions of a man who was looking to just scratch an itch. Sometimes age didn't matter when it came to love. It didn't matter with the judge and me, and maybe it hadn't mattered with Glen and Carly either.

Except if Carly had been interested in Glen, then he wouldn't have had any reason to kill her.

"But everyone says he's such a nice guy, who loved his wife," Molly said, returning to the topic. "Everyone says he's lonely. I get that he might have attached himself to Carly, maybe not as a romantic interest but as a fatherly, or grand-fatherly, figure, but I can't see him killing her."

"You said it yourself that sometimes people who stalk and kill are the folks you'd be least likely to suspect," I pointed out.

"I didn't really know him either," J.T. chimed in. "I tend to buy my fruit and produce from the grocery store. Jellies and pies as well, but I have been out to the orchard a few times each year to pick up a few items. I don't remember ever seeing him, or any of the family, though."

"Bert said Glen and his wife did a lot in the community, but after her death he wasn't really active outside of his business and family," I told him. "But that's not particularly odd. Lots of people stop participating in community stuff when they're grieving, and it could have been that his wife was the driving force in all of that."

J.T. nodded. "I wonder why he did it? Why would he kill a twenty-year-old woman who worked for him? I just don't get the crime-of-passion vibe from this."

That was my question as well. Why would a man in his early sixties, someone committed to his business and his family, murder a twenty-year-old woman?

"She was supposedly pretty," Molly commented. "The picture her parents sent out for the missing person's flyers was from her high school senior photo, and she *was* really pretty. Maybe he knew she wouldn't be interested in an old guy like him, so he just grabbed her. Then he had to kill her so he wouldn't get caught and go to jail."

"Again, early sixties, Molly," I told her with a mock scowl. "Not old."

"She has a point though, aside from the whole 'old' thing," J.T. said. "Maybe he was infatuated with her."

"He was keeping her skull in his attic, so that does mesh with the whole infatuation thing," Molly agreed.

"I don't know." I frowned at my notes. "Maybe he's got the rest of her up in the attic in other boxes, and the one with the skull just happened to be the one Elise grabbed to donate. Maybe it was less about infatuation and more about a safe space for her remains where no one would find them."

J.T.'s eyebrows lifted. "What other motive could he have had besides infatuation? He was in his early sixties. She was in her twenties. You said he was a widower, that the loss of his wife devastated him. Even if he's not a serial killer, he could have snapped after his wife died. Perhaps Carly looked like his wife when she was young, and he went kinda nuts. Couldn't help himself."

"Or he caught her stealing, confronted her and accidently killed her. Then he freaked out and did what he did to cover up the crime." I frowned, because pulling off to the side of the road and ambushing a young woman on her way to her job didn't seem like a reasonable way to confront someone for stealing.

"Or she caught him doing something illegal and threatened to report him," I said, thinking of something more plausible. "So he killed her to keep her silent. Or they were having a consensual affair and she wanted to go public, but he didn't want the scandal or his family to know. Or she truly did have an accident, drove off the road and died, and he covered it up because the orchard could have been sued or been held negligent for some reason." I ticked the scenarios off on my fingers.

"I can't see how the orchard would have been liable for an auto accident," Molly countered. "And what the heck would he have been doing that was illegal? Selling counterfeit apples? Smuggling heroin in the pies? As for Carly stealing, nothing we've uncovered about her so far would point to that. The woman was working three jobs, and everyone who knew her said she was hardworking and honest."

"The orchard was in financial trouble," J.T. pointed out. "Maybe the heroin-in-the-pie thing isn't so farfetched."

I laughed. "You just want it to be heroin-in-the-pie because that would make for a good YouTube episode!"

J.T. grinned and held up his hands. "Guilty as charged."

"Maybe he was keeping customer's credit card info and selling it to identity thief rings," Molly suggested. "Carly found out, confronted him, and he killed her."

I blew out a breath. "Either way, Glen McCray is my main suspect. I called Detective Keeler on my way in and told him everything I knew. So hopefully the police will be able to add in the information they have to what I've provided and connect the dots."

Molly and J.T. offered similar hopes, then we all turned back to the work that paid the bills. I stayed a little later than them, trying to get caught up enough that I wouldn't have to do too much tonight. Judge Beck had taken Cagney on walks for the last two evenings, and I really wanted to do my part tonight, or at least go with him on the walk rather than stay behind, frantically trying to get work done.

Just before I packed up for the day, I searched the obituary listings for Carol McCray. When I pulled up the notice, I enlarged the picture, putting it side-by-side with one of Carly Billings.

Carol's obituary photo was from her wedding. It showed a radiant, bright-eyed, fresh-faced young woman with long light brown hair and a wide smile. I looked back and forth between that picture and the one from Carly's missing-person's report, and noted the similarities. The two women weren't twins, but they had the same wide smile, the same kind eyes, the same long, straight, light brown hair.

Carly looked like could have been Carol's sister, age

differences aside. I could see how a grieving man would look at her and remember his beloved wife. I could see how he would look at Carly, and maybe hope for something the young woman wasn't prepared to give.

CHAPTER 24

Taco greeted me at the door, but Cagney was nowhere to be seen. I had a moment of panic, then saw that her leash was missing from the hook beside the door and that there was a note on the foyer table from the judge.

Went for a walk with the dog. Be home soon.

After letting Taco out for his evening stroll, I headed to the kitchen to check on the stew I'd put in the Crockpot this morning before leaving for work. Everything was starting to fall into a groove schedule-wise, and I really enjoyed it. The dog. Dinner. Post-dinner relaxation. Bedtime. Judge Beck and I had one set of routines for when the kids were here, and one for when they weren't, and adding Cagney had only meant some minor shifting.

The stew smelled amazing, so I went ahead and set the table, put some Italian bread in the oven to warm, and got out a bottle of wine. Hearing the front door open, I went back to the foyer and saw the judge, Cagney, and Taco coming inside. Judge Beck unhooked Cagney and she ran over to growl and bark at the witch.

189

I grimaced, not happy with this habit of hers. The dog couldn't walk past the thing without barking at it. When Henry came back on Sunday, we were going to have to insist that he take it up to his room.

Just then Taco jumped up on the stair railing, then took a leap to land right on top of the witch, smashing her pointed hat. The thing came to life, eyes glowing and hands waving as she cackled.

I just about jumped out of my skin. Cagney yelped, then took off for the kitchen with her tail between her legs. The only one unbothered by the witch was Taco who settled in on top of her hat and surveyed his surroundings.

My heart still pounding, I walked over and unplugged the witch. "Okay. This thing has got to go."

"Henry and I will take it up to his room as soon as he gets here on Sunday," the judge promised.

With the sudden silence, Cagney poked her head out from the kitchen, then began barking again at the witch, her ears pinned back and her eyes wide.

I pointed to the dog. "We'll never get her to walk through the foyer again as long as this is still here. Can't the two of us manage to get it upstairs tonight?"

As if knowing her courage was in question, Cagney dashed forward, biting the witch's black gauzy dress and growling. She shook her head, backing up, and the thing toppled forward. Taco jumped from his perch, landing with a thump on the foyer table before sliding across it and falling to the floor, thankfully landing on his feet.

The witch didn't fare so well. She crashed to the ground, nearly taking the judge with her and sending Cagney yelping back into the kitchen.

"I've got it." Judge Beck bent down to pick up the witch just as Cagney, with another display of courage, raced in to bite and hold the thing's arm. The doorbell rang just as the judge and Cagney began a rather loud tug of war, the growls punctuated by shouts of "Cagney, no!" and "Leave it!"

I opened the door to see Detective Keeler on the other side. He took one look at what was going on in my foyer and his eyes widened.

"Uh, is this a bad time?" he asked.

"No, it's not," the judge yelled. "Keeler. Get in here and help me get this thing upstairs. Cagney, sit! Cut it out."

I couldn't imagine the detective taking orders from anyone, but he dropped the briefcase he was carrying, raced through the door, and grabbed the witch's legs while I tried to pull Cagney off it, alternating threats and bribes of treats. I finally managed to separate Cagney from the witch and held the pup by the collar as the judge and the detective wrestled the witch up the stairs. Judge Beck had a few choice words for his son's latest acquisition as they had to lift it up and over the banister at the first turn, but Detective Keeler remained silent.

As soon as they were out of sight, Cagney was willing to be distracted with a chew-bone. I put her in the powder room with the gate across the opening, just in case she decided the men needed rescuing from the witch, and waited at the bottom of the stairs for them to return.

"I'm sorry about that," I told the detective once he and the judge were back downstairs. "Was it me you were here to see, or Judge Beck?"

"You, actually, Mrs. Carrera." He sniffed. "Am I disturbing your dinner hour? I can come back."

"Nonsense Detective Keeler." Judge Beck slapped the other man on the shoulder. "Stay for dinner. Kay made stew."

The detective eyed the door as if he were counting the steps and wondering how fast he could escape. "Oh, I couldn't. Thank you, but I'll just come back."

"It's really no trouble," I assured him. "Actually it's the

least we can do after making you lug a six-foot animatronic witch up two flights of stairs. I'm sure that wasn't on your list of activities for the evening."

His lips twitched. "No, it wasn't. If you insist, I'll join your for dinner. After, can we go over what you said in your voice mail? I just want to get all the information down so I can follow up."

"We can do that during dinner," I told him. "Judge Beck and I often work during the evenings or while eating. It's not like we're having a fancy meal or anything."

I quickly set another place at the table for the detective, then left the judge to entertain while I put the stew into a tureen and took the bread out of the oven. Within minutes, we were seated and enjoying our meal, Detective Keeler opting for water instead of the wine the judge and I were having. As we ate, the detective went over all I'd told him on the message I'd left. He jotted down the contact information for Bridget and Halley, and asked how positive Bert was that the box came from the McCray house.

"He didn't look through the boxes, but he's sure they all had the orchard logo on them," I confirmed. "And Elise, the granddaughter who gave him the donations, said they were dishes and holiday decorations."

I squirmed a little, not sure if it was enough for Keeler to act on. My word that I "was pretty sure" the box with the skull had arrived on Thursday due to where it was stacked in the house. Kat's and Henry's word that the box had the name of a produce company and their logo on it, that Henry was "pretty sure" the logo was an apple and that the company was an orchard starting with "Mc". Bert being "pretty sure" that the boxes he'd picked up from the McCray house had both the logo, and that he was told there were holiday decorations in at least one of them.

Altogether, it added up, but I was worried that a defense

attorney would pick it all apart one-by-one and cast doubt on each of our statements.

"Did you get the DNA results in yet?" I asked him. "Was the skull Carly's?"

He nodded. "We're still awaiting some further lab tests, but it's definitely her skull. It appears she was killed soon after she went missing, was buried, and was exhumed fairly recently. We've notified her family, but that's it. And we've moved her missing-person's investigation to a homicide, and from a cold case to an active one."

I bet Toots was thrilled with that. I was thrilled—not thrilled that a young woman had died, but that her family finally knew she was gone, and could hope that the investigation would put her killer behind bars.

"Then you might be interested in this." I got up and retrieved the map from my bag, showing him the areas I thought it was likely that Carly had been either abducted or murdered.

"This section of Route 16 is not well traveled," I told him. "Most people turn right out of the orchard to get back to the main road. Carly would have turned left because it was the shortest route to the diner. No one left after her, but someone who knew her routine could have left *before* her and lay in wait at one of these spots. If she knew them and they looked like they were in trouble, she would probably have stopped."

"And you think that someone was Glen McCray?" Keeler asked.

"He *always* left a bit before closing to take the bank deposit in. If he'd turned left instead of right toward the bank, I'm not sure anyone would have noticed. I doubt anyone paid attention to him at all, since this was in keeping with his regular routine."

Keeler pointed to the spots on the map. "Or someone else

could have lay in wait here. A stalker that knew her schedule. Someone from the diner that knew her schedule and the other places she worked. Or even one of these farmers who might have regularly seen her drive to the diner from their fields."

"But her skull wasn't found in a box of Halloween decorations in the attic of any of their houses," I pointed out. "It was found in Glen McCray's house."

"During the initial investigation, the boyfriend had claimed Carly had broken up with him to be with another man." Keeler shook his head. "He didn't know details about this alleged rival boyfriend, and both her closest friends and family had no idea there was a second man in the wings, so we assumed the boyfriend was trying to divert suspicion away from himself."

I nodded in agreement, thinking that if there had been a rival boyfriend, Hally at least would have known about it. Why keep it secret? And none of that fit with my theory that Glen, obsessed with Carly, killed her rather than let her leave with Memphis to Florida.

My phone beeped and I glanced at the text, paying more attention when I found it was from Molly. Molly, who was far more obsessed with the Carly Billings case than I ever gave her credit for. Molly, who was seriously showing a lot of skill at being a future investigator.

"About ten acres of the orchard was sold last year to a developer who is preparing to break ground in the next month according to his permits," I told Keeler. "That might have been what forced Glen to move the body. It might have been safer and less risky to carry the bones to his house and hide them in assorted boxes in the attic than re-bury them elsewhere."

Then I saw the rest of Molly's text and gasped. I had no

idea how she'd managed to dig this information up, but the girl seriously needed a raise.

"Carly had accepted admission to the nursing college. She was due to start that fall, and her first semester was paid in full." I turned to Keeler. "The girl only had three hundred dollars in her account when she vanished. She didn't make enough to pay her tuition up front, and there was nothing on her credit reports about taking out loans."

Keeler held up his hands. "So, grants? Scholarships?"

I waved my phone at him. "No, a check from Glen McCray. One big check. They partially refunded him when she didn't show in the fall."

The detective whistled. "I'll have to confirm with the college, but that's big."

It was big, but was it enough?

"Her skull in a box in his attic," I said, ticking the items off my fingers. "She worked for him. He had opportunity to grab her the night of her disappearance. And he paid her tuition in full. Glen McCray isn't a rich man. The orchard has been struggling for years, and this couldn't have just been the generosity of a wealthy boss. He was obsessed with Carly, and when paying her college didn't convince her to leave her boyfriend for him, he killed her."

"It's not enough to convince a jury beyond a reasonable doubt," Judge Beck chimed in, listening to our conversation with rapt attention. "But it's a good start, and you might be able to find enough information to build a case. Love letters. Texts. The rest of her body and a cause of death would definitely help."

"Think it's enough to get a warrant to search the house?" Keeler asked the judge. "And the store and orchard, if that's not pushing it? Off the record," he added hastily.

"The skull, the word of several people that connects the skull to the house," the judge mused. "Proximity, since she worked for them. Plus the college tuition payment. I might be convinced to sign off on a search warrant. Although in reality I'd have to send you to a different judge. My involvement in the case, although in a non-official capacity, would make it improper for me to sign the warrant."

Detective Keeler grimaced. "I understand, Your Honor. And I appreciate your dedication to avoiding any potential conflict of interest."

"Brownnoser," I mouthed silently, turning my head so he couldn't read my lips.

"Not that I want to stick my nose further into the investigation, but I'd be concerned that if the rest of the bones were in the attic, they may have been moved by now." The judge got up and began to pick up the bowls, waving Keeler away as he rose to help.

"I agree," I said. "Bert's car was broken into Thursday night, so clearly either Glen or his daughter were trying to get to the box before the skull was discovered. I'm assuming one of them was behind the break-in of my garage Friday night as well. Amanda was at the yard sale Sunday asking me about Halloween decorations, and then I spoke to her this week and questioned her about Carly Billings under the guise of working for the girl's parents. She must know the skull was found, and that at the very least, I'm making connections."

"I'm glad that security system is being installed tomorrow," the judge told me. "I want you to be careful, Kay."

I nodded, although I didn't think I was in any danger. The killer was a man slightly older than me who was still dealing with the effects of a serious stroke. And as for Amanda, I was pretty sure she was just helping her father. Covering up for him was still a crime, but I didn't think she'd compound her involvement by trying to take me out.

"I'd still want to search the house for other evidence,"

Keeler said. "Although you're right and the rest of the bones have probably been moved, I don't think they would just be dumped somewhere. The killer would want to keep them close, where they'd have some control over the area and there would be less chance of someone randomly finding them. I'm hoping I can convince a judge to allow us to search the store and the orchard as well. Although as large as that farm is, it won't be quick or easy. I wish there was some way of narrowing down the possible re-burial area."

A shadowy spirit appeared in the corner of the room. I heard a thump from the kitchen and knew without even seeing it that an apple was now rolling across my island counter.

There were probably lots of freshly dug areas in the orchard, from mulching around the trees, to planting new ones, to digging up old and diseased ones. But I had an idea of who might know exactly where the bones were, and it wasn't just the killer.

CHAPTER 25

I woke early after a fitful night occupied with thoughts of Carly Billings and Glen McCray.

Something didn't feel right. I was beginning to wonder if I'd jumped to conclusions and had made some wrong assumptions about both the victim and the man I'd labeled her killer.

Giving up on sleep, I slipped out of the judge's bed and snuck back to my room to dress. Then I went downstairs and made several batches of butter rum and currant scones before Daisy arrived for yoga.

I was distracted during our morning exercise and Daisy's and my quick coffee-and-scone break. Grabbing a shower and getting ready for work, I boxed up half a dozen scones, kissed the judge, and left him to deal with the security installation people who were just pulling into the driveway as I was pulling out.

Instead of heading to work, I drove to Bert's subdivision, seeing a familiar form on the porch across the street from my friend. Checking his driveway to make sure that Amanda and Elise had left for the day, I pulled up to the curb and got out, grabbing my bag and the half-dozen scones.

"Hi Mr. McCray," I said as I climbed the porch steps. "I'm Kay Carrera and a friend of Bert Peter. From across the street?"

He nodded. "I know Bert. Is he okay?"

"He's fine. But he told me about you and I thought maybe I'd bring you some scones. I made them fresh this morning. They're butter rum and currant."

His eyes lit up. "Oh, I would love some. My wife Carol was such a good baker. I've missed her pies and muffins. Thank you for thinking of me."

"Of course." I felt a bit guilty about my ulterior motive, but set the scones down on the little table beside his chair.

"While I'm here, I'm wondering if I could ask you a few questions about Carly Billings."

It was the worse segue ever. Normally I was pretty good at this sort of thing, but I'd been unable to think of a smooth way to transition from "I'm bringing you some scones" to "I want to question you about a woman you may or may not have murdered."

Glen McCray sighed. His eyes were sad as they met mine. "Carly Billings. Did they ever find her? All these years I've wondered what happened to her. I've prayed that somehow she was okay, even though I feared the worst. Is she...?"

His speech was slow and slurred, but he formed each word carefully. I hesitated a bit before answering him, not sure how to tell him but not tell him, since the detective hadn't released the news to the public yet.

"There's nothing official, but the police have found remains that they believe might be hers," I finally said.

Tears sprang to his eyes. His mouth trembled and he motioned for me to sit in the vacant chair next to him.

"Can you tell me about your relationship with her?" I

asked as I lowered myself into the seat. "I know she worked for you, that you spoke together often."

I held back on the other things I knew, wanting him to tell me those himself.

A brief smile twisted one side of his mouth upward. "I offered to marry her."

That I hadn't expected.

"She was kind and lively and we became friends," he continued. "I used to eat at the diner when she worked nights there. And sometimes she would come over and we would play cards. She wanted to go to nursing school, to have a better life for herself. And I was lonely. She felt trapped, and in some ways I did too."

"You proposed to her?" I was still a little stunned by that.

He nodded. "What we had wasn't physical. I offered friendship, comfort, and security in exchange for companionship. I told her I would pay for her nursing school and everything else she wanted or needed—as long as it was within my somewhat limited means. And we would just be happy together. Comfortable. I would no longer be alone, and she would no longer have to struggle for the basic necessities in life. And she would get the degree, the career, she'd always wanted."

"What did she say when you proposed?" I asked.

Glen lifted one shoulder. "At first, she said she needed to think about it. But a few days before she left…or disappeared, she told me yes. I gave her a ring. I sent in the deposit for the nursing school so she could start in the fall. We planned to exchange vows at the courthouse the next week. When she didn't show up to work that one day and didn't return my calls, I thought maybe she had changed her mind and left with her boyfriend instead. I thought maybe she was too embarrassed to tell me to my face that she no longer wanted to marry me."

"When was the last time you saw her?" I wondered.

"The night she vanished. I left the store to take the deposit to the bank just before she left to go to her job at the diner." His mouth trembled again. "When I saw in the paper that she was actually missing, that they had found her car abandoned... I always thought maybe her boyfriend had killed her when she told him she was marrying me. She said he wasn't the jealous type, but who else could it have been? It's always the boyfriend, isn't it?"

I reached over to squeeze his hand, my mind racing. I'd begun to suspect Glen wasn't the murderer. But the skull was in his house, in his attic. I'd assumed he'd enlisted his daughter's help to cover up the crime, but now—

Amanda. It was Amanda.

"Did your daughter know you were going to marry Carly?" I asked Glen.

He nodded. "She wasn't happy about it. Thought I was making a fool of myself with a girl young enough to be my granddaughter. She didn't want a stepmother that young, or any stepmother at all. I told her this had nothing to do with her, that I just was lonely and wanted companionship."

"Was she angry?" I pressed, rethinking everything I'd discovered to this point.

"Yes, but I know she would have gotten over it." Glen looked over at me. "Amanda is a good girl. Loyal. Hardworking. Dedicated to her family and the business."

"And what was Amanda doing that night?" I pressed. "The night that Carly didn't show up at the diner for work? The night she went missing?"

"Work, as always." Glen sighed. "She said there were some diseased trees she needed to dig up and remove, then something in the barn needed repair. I remember because I had to go to her house and watch Elise. My granddaughter was thirteen, but Amanda didn't like her being home alone after dark. I remember I was there past midnight—not that it's unusual for Amanda to work that late."

Midnight. Digging up trees in the dark and working in the barn. It was *Amanda* who'd killed Carly, not Glen. But like before, I just didn't have enough evidence to prove it.

"When I thought Carly had left with her boyfriend, the one thing I did feel bad about was the ring," Glen said. "I'd given her the engagement ring I'd given to Carol. A little emerald-cut ruby flanked on either side with three diamond chips. It wasn't worth much, but it had personal value. I should have bought something new for her and kept the ring for Elise as a graduation gift, but I guess I'm a sentimental fool. Sometimes I trust people I shouldn't. But I was right to trust Carly. I hope that whoever murdered her and stole that ring gets what's coming to him."

"I worked with Bert on that charity yard sale he was collecting donated items for," I said, once again wincing at my abrupt change of topics. "I really appreciate the dishes and the decorations. The Halloween decorations were a big hit."

He frowned. "Amanda was so upset about that. She's been under a lot of stress lately, but I really didn't understand what the problem was. And it wasn't Elise's fault. I was the one who told her to go up in the attic and give those boxes to Bert. It wasn't like I'd used those dishes or those decorations for years, and I thought it was better for them to go to charity than sit here in dusty boxes."

"You told her which boxes to give to Bert?" I clarified.

He nodded. "There's nothing of value in that attic, but I didn't want Elise spending hours hauling stuff down, and I wasn't sure your charity wanted *that* many donations. I'm glad the Halloween stuff sold. Carol and I used to have fun decorating for holidays. I think there was a jar of fake eyeballs in there, and some fake bones. I didn't realize

Amanda would be so attached to that stuff. I won't give any more things away until I ask her if she wants them. She hasn't had an easy life between Elise's father taking off, Carol dying, raising a daughter as a single mom, and my stroke. I don't want to cause her any more stress."

"Has Amanda expressed interest in any other boxes in the attic?" I asked him.

"She's been going through them," he assured me. "It'll take her forever, but I told her she needed to decide what she wanted and what she didn't, so we could get rid of stuff. Now that the three of us are living here, I'd like to make room for everything. Although Elise is making noises about going to New York, so it might soon just be Amanda and me."

I thought once more about my discussion last night with Keeler, Glen's words reinforcing my belief that the bones had been moved again, just in case the house was searched.

"She took a few boxes out yesterday morning," Glen added. "Probably to keep at the store in case I accidently try to give them away. I don't blame her. I struggle to remember things after the stroke. Amanda was always the one who took care of things, even when Carol was alive. While we were working the store, the cider presses, the preserve and pie making, she was out in the fields taking care of the trees and ensuring the harvest came in. I feel bad that she's always worked so hard. That's why I sold off ten acres of the orchard last year. Amanda was mad at me for that, but I wanted to pay all of our debt off, so she would have the whole business debt-free. I didn't want her encumbered by Carol's and my financial mistakes any longer.

I nodded, barely hearing him. Amanda had been in the fields every day. No one would ever have questioned her coming and going, and she could have easily been in two of the three spots I'd selected as ideal for ambush. Carly would have known her, would have stopped to help if it looked like she was in trouble, or hurt from a farming accident.

Amanda had access to the farm equipment to move Carly's car, to hide it in a barn or outbuilding, and to easily and quickly bury the body. And she would have been able to dig up and relocate the body once she'd realized her father had sold the land it had been buried on.

"Glen, could you give me and the police your permission to look through the store and the orchard? And to search your house? There might be something here or there, some clue that might help us find Carly's killer."

I felt bad for manipulating a man who'd just told me he often trusted the wrong people, but if I was right, then he needed to know what his daughter had done. He needed to know.

Glen smiled over at me. "Of course. I have nothing to hide. And I want to know what happened to Carly. Whoever killed her, I want that person caught. I want them to go to jail. And if there's something in my house or business that can help, then I'm happy to cooperate with the police."

* * *

LESS THAN THIRTY MINUTES LATER, Keeler had officers at Glen McCray's house, once more securing his permission to search his home and business. Then Keeler left his crew to go through the house, coming to meet me at the orchard.

Amanda was furious. She followed Keeler around, protesting the invasion of her family's privacy, and demanding a search warrant. After being told that her father had consented to the search, she ranted that Glen was senile, that he was unable to make his own decisions and that he'd been taken advantage of by dishonest law enforcement officials. She vowed to sue us all—me included.

Elise stood by, horrified by her mother's display.

"Mom, who cares if they look through a bunch of jam jars and cider presses," she said, frantically trying to calm the other woman. "And as for granddad's house, it's his to do with what he wants. Why are the cops even looking through stuff? It's not like they're going to find anything. We've got nothing to hide."

Little did she know they had plenty to hide.

Keeler, and a small group of deputies and officers that included Miles went outside, with the detective and me in the lead and Amanda following, still issuing threats of lawsuits.

"Okay, Mrs. Carrera. Work your magic." Keeler gestured toward the rows of fruit trees that extended to the horizon. "Save us some time here."

"I'm calling my lawyer," Amanda snapped, spinning on her heels to go back inside.

"Seriously, Mrs. Carrera," Keeler pleaded. "We're about an hour tops from getting shut down and needing to wait for an official warrant."

I took a deep breath, and as hoped, the shadowy form of a ghost appeared at the corner of my sight.

Show us where you are, I silently pleaded.

Carly must have sensed the urgency in the situation because the shadow flitted down a row of apple trees. I broke into a jog, moving fast enough to not lose sight of the ghost, but not so fast that it appeared I didn't know where I was going.

I'd expected the ghost to lead us deep into the orchard, to a spot where new trees had been planted or old ones dug up. Instead she guided us around behind one of the outbuildings, past a mulch pile to a stack of old, fungi-covered fruit trees. They looked like they were stacked to dry, and to eventually burn. The ghost hovered over the dead trees, then extended a misty arm toward one section.

"Dig there," I told Keeler and the others.

They dove in, carefully moving trees, limbs, and brush. And ten minutes later, they'd found a neat pile of bones.

CHAPTER 26

I was putting the wine into the ice bucket on the porch, Cagney tethered to one of the support pillars and Taco milling about the boxwoods lining the walkway in search of bugs to pounce on. It seemed like just yesterday we'd all been crammed inside my house, sorting and pricing donations for the charity yard sale. This week's Friday happy-hour-on-the-porch was back to our normal routine, with snacks and wine and no forced labor for the attendees.

"Should I bring out the sausage-things now, or later?" Judge Beck asked as he set a Crockpot full of spicy meatballs on the table next to a covered plate of cheese.

"Let's wait until people start to arrive." The "sausage-things" were sausage links in crescent rolls that had been liberally coated with butter, parmesan, and oregano before they were rolled up. It was something my mother had made for cocktail parties back in the '70s and were still appreciated, unlike the savory gelatin molds or pickled ham salad from the same era.

"Then I'll go ahead and bring out the beer." He went back into the house to get the beverage that he and Matt preferred over the wine or sodas we always put out.

It had been a good week—for us, but not for the McCray family. The search of the house had revealed nothing in the attic aside for some boxes that looked like they'd been hurriedly gone through. The police had found a ring in Amanda's jewelry box though—a ring with a small emerald-cut ruby flanked on either side with three diamond chips. Keeler had shown it to Glen, who'd collapsed in tears, unable to do more than confirm that this was the ring he'd given to his wife, Carol. The same ring he'd given to Carly Billings when she'd agreed to marry him. The last time he'd seen it, it had been on her pinky finger the night she'd vanished, needing to be resized before it would fit on the appropriate digit for an engagement ring.

There was only one way Amanda could have had that ring.

In addition to the bones hidden under the dead trees— bones immediately identified as human and, no doubt, soon to be identified as Carly's—the police had also found scraps of her clothing and broken bits of what had once been a cell phone in the area of land that had been sold to the developer.

They'd also found another body buried near the equipment barn—the body of a man. It appeared to have been there for well over a decade, and I suspected that it might be the body of Elise's father.

It was terrifying that a cold-blooded killer had been in our midst, absolutely unsuspected of any crime. Molly was right about psychopaths. It was always the person who neighbors and family and friends least suspected, who everyone would describe as nice and kind, as hardworking, loyal, family-focused. I'd spoken to Amanda, questioned her about Carly Billings's disappearance, and never once got even a hint that she might be capable of murder.

My heart twisted as I thought of Glen. And Elise.

The girl was young, and she had time to recover—as if anyone could ever fully recover from finding out their mother was a murderer. But Glen… What would happen to the orchard? To the store? To him? Elise would probably go to New York as she'd planned, to escape this whole nightmare and attempt to reinvent herself. But what about Glen? Would he ever recover from this? His wife gone. His daughter gone. His granddaughter, most likely gone. Who would he turn to for the love and companionship he craved?

He seemed so old when I'd spoken to him, but in reality Glen was only seven or eight years older than me. He was still young. And I'd found love and companionship—in a younger man. The irony wasn't lost on me, although Judge Beck wasn't young enough to be my son or grandson, there still was an unusual age gap between us. At least, it was unusual when the woman was the older partner.

I felt so young, while Glen seemed so old. Was age really just a state of mind? Or had my friends, my connections, kept that youth alive in me? Had my relationship with Judge Beck really taken twenty years off my age, as Daisy had suggested? Maybe not literally in terms of my physical appearance, but instead in terms of my attitude and energy?

It certainly felt that way.

I laughed, wondering if the key to everlasting youth was a younger boyfriend. Or maybe sex. Or maybe just having people that loved you and cared enough to show up when you needed them.

As cars pulled up to the curb and people began to walk up the steps to the porch, I made a silent vow to take scones over to Glen McCray every week or so. Play cards with him. Invite a group of friends over so we all could play cards.

Or maybe invite him out somewhere to play cards, or bingo, or drink wine on a porch on Friday night. Bert had promised to come to our happy hours. I could ask him to pick Glen up and bring him along.

Everyone needs friends, I thought as the judge came out with the cooler full of beer.

Just then I heard something thump upstairs and the faint sound of an electronic witch cackling. Cagney began to howl. Judge Beck and I exchanged a quick smile, then he ran back inside, presumably to unplug the troublesome witch.

Yes, everyone needed friends. And if we got a little more than friends later in life when we didn't expect it? Well then, so much the better.

* * *

WANT MORE STORIES ABOUT KAY, Judge Beck, and friends? Join my newsletter and never miss a new release, plus get updates on sales, recipes, and more! The next book in the Locust Point Mystery Series, Lonely Hearts, is up next. Information and preorder links are coming soon!

ABOUT THE AUTHOR

Libby Howard lives in a little house in the woods with her sons and two exuberant bloodhounds. She occasionally knits, occasionally bakes, and occasionally manages to do a load of laundry. Most of her writing is done in a bar where she can combine work with people-watching, a decent micro-brew, and a plate of Old Bay wings.

For more information:
libbyhowardbooks.com/

ACKNOWLEDGMENTS

Special thanks to Lyndsey Lewellen for cover design and Kimberly Cannon for editing.

In memory of my mother who was my biggest fan and my partner-in-crime.